I'll Sing for my Dinner

By BR Kingsolver

Cover art by Mia Darien

http://www.miadarien.com/

Published by BR Kingsolver

Copyright 2015 BR Kingsolver

~~~

ACKNOWLEDGEMENTS

Valentina, as always, for your time, encouragement and edits. Mia Darien for the cover art, edits, comments and suggestions. A special thanks to Alicia, Alexandra, Angela, Cassie, Christy, Chelsea, Gretchen, Jackie, Jane, Jenna, Jolene, Rebecca (Bec), and Toni for reading my drafts and offering advice for some very difficult material. The book is much better due to your help. To all of you, a sincere thank you.

Previous books by BR Kingsolver
The Succubus Gift
Succubus Unleashed
Broken Dolls
Succubus Rising
Succubus Ascendant
Gifts of the Goddess: The complete Telepathic Clans Saga
Trust: a truly modern romance

License Notes

This ebook is licensed for your personal enjoyment only. This ebook may not be re-sold or given away to other people. If you would like to share this book with another person, please purchase an additional copy for each recipient. If you're reading this book and did not purchase it, or it was not purchased for your use only, then please return it and purchase your own copy. Thank you for respecting the hard work of this author.

Contents

Chapter 1 1
Chapter 2 10
Chapter 3 17
Chapter 4 25
Chapter 5 34
Chapter 6 44
Chapter 7 53
Chapter 8 59
Chapter 9 64
Chapter 10 74
Chapter 11 82
Chapter 12 89
Chapter 13 91
Chapter 14 96
Chapter 15 100
Chapter 16 108
Chapter 17 113
Chapter 18 122
Chapter 19 127
Chapter 20 131
Chapter 21 139
Chapter 22 147
Chapter 23 156
Chapter 24 158
Chapter 25 167
Chapter 26 170
Chapter 27 172
Chapter 28 176

Chapter 29	181
Chapter 30	185
Chapter 31	193
Chapter 32	197

I'll Sing for my Dinner

Chapter 1

Jake

A pickup truck pulled up in front of the bar and stopped. It looked like Luke Sowers in the driver's seat. The door on the other side opened, but I couldn't see who got out. Then the truck pulled out again, the tires throwing gravel, and sped off.

What was left, standing in the parking lot, looked like a hippie. A girl, with a backpack and something else. She shouldered the pack, picked up what I now could see was a guitar case, and headed for the door. Apparently, she was a hitchhiker and he dropped her off at my place. Thanks, Luke.

Making her way through the door, she came straight toward me instead of taking a seat at one of the tables. The sign by the door said 'Seat yourself,' so I wondered what in the hell this was all about.

Stopping in front of me, she looked up into my face and asked in one of the most beautiful voices I'd ever heard, "May I speak to the owner, or the manager?"

The voice was a surprise, like a flower blooming in the desert. Her face was a shock. For all the grime, she was beautiful. Not pretty, but the kind of beauty you see on the covers of magazines. Long stringy greasy hair fell past her small breasts. She was thin, too thin, with a look in her gray eyes I hadn't seen since coming back to the States, a combination of shell shock and hunger. The overall impression she projected was fragility. She came up to about my shoulder and I wasn't sure she was old enough to be in a bar. What in the hell was she doing hitchhiking alone?

"I'm the owner, and the manager," I replied. "I'm Jake McGarrity."

"I'm Cecily," she said. Turning, she looked around the room. The Roadhouse is a pretty typical bar with a bandstand at the end opposite the door and an area cleared for dancing. It was six-thirty in the evening, and we had two families with kids, about half a dozen couples, and two groups of four cowboys, all eating dinner. On a Wednesday night, that was pretty good. On a weekend, we did a lot better, and lunch was usually packed.

Turning back to me, she licked her lips and then said, "You have live music in here." It was a statement, not a question. I nodded. The bandstand with the microphones and amplifiers made that pretty obvious.

"We have a band start at nine on Thursday, Friday and Saturday nights," I said.

"Do you ever have live music for your dinner guests?"

I gestured to one of the speakers on the wall. "We use canned music."

"Mr. McGarrity, I don't have a red cent to my name, and I haven't eaten in two days," she said. "I'll play for your guests in exchange for a meal."

My God. The raw, naked hope in her face was almost too much for me. My eyes blurred a little bit. People tell me sometimes that I'm a soft touch. I figure that charity never hurts the giver. I was going to feed her. There was no way I was going to turn someone away after they approached me like that.

"What kind of music do you play?" I asked.

She shrugged. "I can play anything. For dinner music," she gestured toward the customers sitting at the tables, "something soft and relaxing, loud enough to be noticed, but not so loud that people can't carry on a conversation. People's behavior is different with live music, you know.

They stay longer after they finish their meals and order more drinks."

In addition to the beauty of her voice, her accent was cultured. This girl was raised with money, or at least well educated. And she hadn't been on the streets long enough for her vocabulary to degenerate. She didn't even speak like a normal kid.

I took a deep breath, and then she said in a rush, "Let me just play a couple of songs. Okay? Before you decide. Please? And then, if you don't think it's a good idea, I'll go."

Go where? Go out and stand beside the highway with her thumb out? Just the thought of her hitchhiking, getting in strangers' cars and ending the night raped and dead in a ditch, scared the hell out of me. If I read about her in the newspaper tomorrow, I'd never be able to forgive myself.

Nodding, I said, "Let's hear what you've got." I pulled a menu out from under the bar and pushed it across to her. "Give me your order, and you can play until your food is ready."

Looking down the menu, she raised her head. "I don't want you to think I'm taking advantage. Could I get the baked flounder and a salad? Is that too much?"

"What kind of dressing on your salad?" I answered.

"Oil and vinegar, or Italian. Something like that."

"Put your backpack over there," I said, pointing to a corner behind the bar and off to the side of the kitchen door.

She dropped the pack there, and as she passed me, I got a whiff of her. She and her clothes hadn't been washed in far too long. Taking her guitar case up to the bandstand, she pulled out a beautiful Martin D45 with an electronic pickup. She could hock the guitar for enough money to get anywhere in the country, and eat well besides. The way she handled it, I had a feeling she'd starve to death before that happened.

Plugging into an amp, she checked the tuning on the guitar, flipped on the power, and hit a note. She turned the volume down, pulled a stool up to the edge of the bandstand and sat down.

I watched as she fitted finger picks on her right hand, and I wondered exactly what I was about to hear. All of her movements were efficient, practiced. She had played for audiences before, and she didn't show a shred of nervousness.

I went and turned off the canned music and nodded to her. Most of my customers glanced her way, and some turned and watched her. Everyone was curious. I knew all these folks, and they were good people. Unless she sounded like a tortured cat, they would be polite.

And then she started to play. I recognized the tune immediately. Segovia, played on a steel-string guitar. As she promised, the music filled the room, but it was quiet enough that it wasn't intrusive. I listened in astonishment as she flawlessly negotiated the complex piece of classical music. When she finished, she moved right into a Frank Sinatra tune, and from there a song off an old Mason Williams album. She hadn't been bragging when she said she could play anything.

"You're going to screw up your reputation as a hard-boiled ex-Marine," Kathy said with a chuckle when she brought Cecily's meal from the kitchen, startling me out of some kind of trance I had fallen into watching Cecily play.

"At least she's paying for her meal," Kathy continued. "Normally you just feed down-and-out vets who offer nothing but a hard-luck story."

"I don't have a need to impress people with what kind of hard-ass I am," I told her. "Too many of the guys I knew like that got their asses shot off trying to be a hero."

I waived Cecily over, and she came to the bar and perched on one of the barstools. She ate slowly, carefully chewing small bites. That about broke my heart. She was used to being hungry, and knew wolfing it down might cause her to be sick.

"Would you like something to drink besides water?" I asked.

She gave me a startled look, then looked at the taps and bottles lined up behind the bar. "A glass of white wine would be nice," she said. "Do you pour a sauvignon blanc by the glass?"

Where in the hell did this girl come from? And what happened to her to put her in this kind of personal hell out on the Colorado plains? I poured her wine and set it down in front of her.

She swirled the wine in the glass, smelled it, and took a sip. That earned me an even more startled look.

"Is this really what you normally pour as bar wine?" she asked, her eyes wide.

"It's what I pour for dirty, starving hitchhikers who play Segovia on fine, vintage guitars," I answered. The fact that she recognized the quality of the bottle I'd opened for her told me volumes as to how she used to live.

She blushed. "Thank you."

"Do you sing?" I asked.

"Yes. Is it all right if I sing?"

"Do whatever you like. From what I've heard so far, you've got more than a meal coming if you want to keep playing. I'll pay you fifty bucks to play until eight."

More customers had come in, but none had left. When she walked back onto the stage, everyone quieted and looked toward her expectantly. She started picking an intricate tune that settled into Bob Dylan's *Don't Think Twice, It's All Right*. She opened her mouth, and at the first note every other sound in the bar stopped. Even the noises in the kitchen stopped.

She sang in a strong, clear, pure mezzo-soprano, dropping into the contralto range on the tag line of each verse. Finishing the song, she immediately launched into Joni Mitchell's *Chelsea Morning*, sung soprano, and followed that with Loretta Lynn's *Coal Miner's Daughter*, her voice taking on a twang that would make any hillbilly proud.

On *Chelsea Morning*, she took the notes on the words 'heard' and 'pipes' so high that I nervously glanced at my glassware.

Her voice was flawless, with no reaching for notes, either on the high or low end of any register in which she chose to sing. I had never heard anything like it in my life.

Kathy, my assistant manager, took a glass of water up to the stage around the fourth song and set it next to her on the floor. Two songs later, one of the cowboys came over to the bar.

"Have you got a bowl or something, Jake? She should have a hat or something. You know, something people can put tips in."

"Why don't you loan her your hat, Mel?" I asked him with a grin.

"Hell, Jake, she probably wouldn't want to touch the money after it sat in my sweat all night," he said, grinning back at me. I had to admit, the battered lump of felt sitting on his head had seen better days.

I went back to the kitchen and got a bowl. When I handed it to him, he dropped a dollar in it, then walked back to his table. His friends also dropped money in the bowl, and he took it up and set it on the stage in front of her.

She smiled at him without missing a note. A thousand-watt smile that made him blush.

She played almost solid for over an hour, transitioning from folk to country, to gospel, to blues, even including a Billy Holiday song and a couple from Barbra Streisand. Her vocal range was incredible as she moved effortlessly from soprano to contralto. I don't know how many people in a cowboy honky-tonk bar would recognize a classically-trained voice, but I did.

When she finished, I handed her fifty dollars and said, "If you want to come back, I'll pay you a hundred dollars a night to play and sing between six and eight. Five nights a week, Wednesday through Sunday."

"Seriously?"

"As serious as a heart attack," I said. "Do you know where you're going to spend the night? There's a motel just a block down. It's not fancy, but it's clean."

Looking at the money in her hand, she said, "I can't afford a motel. I have a sleeping bag. I'll find a place to crash." She glanced over her shoulder at the cowboys who started her tip collection. From what I'd seen, she did pretty well on tips. "Maybe someone will offer me a bed."

That did it. I had seen women in Afghanistan who had fallen so far that they were willing to sell their bodies for a scrap to eat or a warm place to sleep. Every protective instinct I had leaped up and opened my mouth.

"You can stay at my place," I said.

She looked at the tattoo on my forearm, then back up to my face. A smile crooked the corners of her mouth, but it didn't change the sad look in her eyes. "I've never slept with a jarhead before."

Shaking my head, I said, "That's not what I'm offering. You can stay in my spare room. It has its own bath. And you can do some laundry."

Looking down at herself, she murmured, "That would be nice." Raising her eyes to my face, she seemed to study me. "Mr. McGarrity, you're too nice for your own good. How do you know I'm not a drug addict that will cut your throat and clean you out before morning?"

"I don't sleep that heavy," I said. "I'll take the chance. As for being too nice, I'm not. No one has ever taken advantage of me twice."

I asked Kathy to cover the bar until I got back. Grabbing her backpack, I said, "Come on, I'll take you over there."

"Don't you have to work?"

"I'll drop you off and come back."

We went out to my pickup and I dumped her pack in the back. She brought the guitar inside with her, settling it on the floor and holding the neck of the case between her legs.

"That's a nice guitar," I said.

"It was my twelfth birthday present."

"It's a D45, isn't it? Rosewood?" I asked, referring to the guitar's body.

"Yes."

The last time I'd seen an older D45 on sale of the quality she was playing, the shop was asking twelve thousand dollars. Someone had loved her to give that to a twelve year old.

"Do you play?" she asked. "You seem to know a lot about guitars."

"Yes, but I'm light years away from your class. I have a D35 at home. My brother's band is our standard house band. They'll be playing tomorrow night."

"Do you play with them?"

"Sometimes. He and I started the band in high school, and he kept it going when I joined the Marines."

She nodded. We rode in silence for a while, then abruptly she said, "Mr. McGarrity, if anyone ever tells me that chivalry is dead, I'm going to send them to the Roadhouse Bar and Grill. It's been a long time since anyone was this nice to me."

Chapter 2
Cecily

McGarrity drove out into the country, away from town. If this was a ride I took out on the highway, I would be reaching for the knife hanging in a sheath between my breasts. I figured that I had offered to sleep with him, and he'd turned me down, at least for the moment. I didn't blame him for that. The way I smelled was probably a pretty good rape deterrent. The guy who picked me up in Fort Morgan and dropped me off at McGarrity's place couldn't wait to get me out of his truck. Probably took it to a carwash to disinfect it the moment he left. Still, no man ever was nice to me without wanting something and lately it seemed what they wanted was between my legs.

Jake McGarrity. I studied him in the soft light of the sun going down behind us. If you looked in the dictionary, his picture might be there right next to the entry for 'ruggedly handsome.' Dark hair cut really short, but longer I'm sure than when he'd been in the service. About six feet tall, well built and athletic looking, but not muscle-bound. He was dressed like all the other men in this part of the country. Pearl snaps on his cowboy shirt, boot-cut blue jeans, and cowboy boots. He'd put on a cowboy hat when we left the bar.

I hadn't known there were cowboy angels, but you learn something new every day. Hell, what would a city girl from the East Coast really know about cowboys? I knew I'd never met an angel before. He didn't look at all like the pictures in Sunday school. I wondered if he lived on a ranch. We definitely had left the city behind.

He seemed kind of young to own a bar. I figured he was around thirty, maybe even a little younger. The Roadhouse was fairly big, located on the corner of two highways with a large parking lot surrounding it. The dance floor would probably accommodate about fifty couples, and I counted seating, including at the bar, for more than three hundred people. A forty-foot-high lighted sign that you could put messages on stood out in front. At the moment, it said, 'Prairie Lightning – Thurs', 'Bluegrass Revolution – Fri & Sat', and at the bottom, 'Steak Special - $19.99 40 oz T-bone.'

I could eat for a week on a forty-ounce steak.

I expected some sign of disapproval from the waitress at the bar, who told me her name was Kathy. Especially when he said that he was taking me home. Up until that point, I had seen pity and sympathy in her face when she looked at me. But she didn't tell him he was crazy, or look at me like I was trash. She just got an amused expression on her face, kind of like a mother looking at a child with a wild but harmless idea. Like it was the kind of thing she expected of him.

I looked around at the pickup. It seemed pretty fancy. It certainly was big. There were three rifles hanging on a rack in the back window. I wondered what he hunted.

We turned off the paved road onto a dirt road. A sign on a fence said, 'Top Hat Ranch', with a pictogram below it that I thought might be a brand. Did they still brand cattle? It looked a bit like a top hat. Another mile along, and we pulled into a large open circle surrounded by buildings. A two-story house with a big white porch sat directly in front of us. A large barn sat to our left, and what looked like another barn, one story high and much longer than it was wide, was on our right. Two or three smaller buildings seemed to be scattered randomly around.

The house was almost as large as my parents' house, the one where I grew up, but as different from theirs as Connecticut was from Colorado. Two dogs waited for us, wagging their tails. One was large and yellow, barking like crazy. The other one was smaller, white and black, and it was spinning around in circles and leaping up in the air.

Jake got out of the truck and was assaulted by the dogs. He petted them and then told them to go lie down. They both ran toward the lower barn and disappeared.

"The big one's Barney," McGarrity said. "The little one is Mari. She's a maniac. Barney's bark is worse than his bite. I'll formally introduce you to them in the morning."

Hauling my pack out of the back of his truck, he led me into the house. A parlor, quaintly decorated, sat to our right as we entered. A dining room and beyond that a kitchen were to the left. We passed through the foyer into a large living room.

Pointing beyond to a narrow hallway leading to the back of the house, he said, "Laundry room is back there."

He headed up the stairs, still carrying my pack as if it weighed nothing. At the top, he pointed to the end of the hall and said, "My room is there." Turning around, he pointed to the other end of the hall. "You'll be staying there."

"Do you live alone?" I asked. He wasn't wearing any rings.

"Just me and my brother, but he usually stays at a girlfriend's place," he answered.

He opened the door, flipped on the light and set my pack in the corner near the foot of the bed. Queen sized, with a heavy dark wood headboard and footboard, it was covered in a lovely crocheted bedspread.

"Bathroom is here," he said, opening a door on our left and switching on the light. "If you take a shower, be sure the curtain is tucked inside. Otherwise, water will be all over the floor and I'll be repairing the ceiling in the kitchen."

He opened another door, and I was surprised to see women's clothing hanging in the closet. "I expect these will be too big for you," he said, "but maybe some of the tops will be okay. At least you'll have something to wear around the house while you wash your clothes." He looked me up and down. "Maybe some of the jeans in the very back will fit, though they'll be too long. You can roll them up. Mary never threw out anything, so stuff from when she was a kid is probably still there." He looked toward a large dresser. "There are more clothes there. Don't be shy about taking what you need."

"Who is Mary?" I asked, suddenly uncomfortable with him putting me in someone else's room.

"She was my sister," he said. "She died three years ago. There is food in the kitchen. I have to get back to work. Do you think you'll be all right here? I'll be home about three o'clock. You don't have to wait up for me."

"I'll be fine." My heart felt like it was about to burst. The whirlwind that gathered me up when I walked into the bar had my head spinning. If you had asked me that morning where I would end up that night, I would have guessed dead in a ditch before I imagined this. "Mr. McGarrity, I don't know what to say. Do you always bring home strays like this?"

He laughed. "I have that tendency, but it's usually limited to dogs, cats, horses, that sort of thing. You're the first girl I've dragged home with me."

I stepped up beside him, and standing on my tiptoes, kissed him on the cheek. "Thank you. You must be the sweetest man God ever made."

He blushed deep red. "Well, I need to get back. Get out of those clothes and throw them and anything you have in your pack in the laundry, then take a bath. Or a shower if you wish." Plucking a bathrobe from the closet, he handed it to me, then turned to leave.

"Okay," I said. "I promise I'll smell better when you get back."

He blushed again. I listened to him going down the stairs, then out the door. "I've locked the door," he shouted. "Don't open it for anyone but me or a man named Jared. And if he comes by, make sure you have some clothes on before you let him in."

I smiled and yelled back, "Dangerous, is he?"

"He's only dangerous if you're susceptible to his blarney," he shouted back. "At least if you have clothes on, it will slow him down."

I heard his pickup start and drive away. Immediately, I stripped to the skin. I didn't even want to touch the bathrobe before I washed. Since I was alone in the house, no one would care if I were naked. Digging through my backpack, I gathered everything that possibly could be washed, and took the clothes downstairs. I followed the hallway he'd pointed out and found myself in a room with the back door. A dog door was cut in it. To my left were a modern washer and dryer sitting under shelves with detergent, fabric softener, and anything else I might need.

Looking around the room, I saw more shelves that held stacks of canned goods, cleaning supplies, and a couple of very large stew pots. A large bowl of water sat on the floor with two smaller empty bowls. I assumed they were for the dogs. Two smaller bowls, one with water and one with dry pet food, sat on a shelf.

The washer was turned to cold water. The health department would probably order most of my clothes burned, but they were all I had. I cranked the temperature switch to hot, measured out detergent, and dumped my clothes in. Separating colors was a joke. Anything I had that used to be white was now gray.

Padding out of the laundry room, I went into the kitchen and opened the refrigerator. It was full of food, along with two different kinds of beer and three bottles of white wine. I had seen a full wine rack in the dining room. Not what I would have expected of a cowboy. A large jug of orange juice, however, riveted my attention. I found a glass and poured it full. Taking a sip, I moaned in pleasure.

Even though the house was obviously pretty old, the paint both outside and inside was well maintained. The kitchen had been upgraded, and not too long before. They had done it right, with granite counters and a large granite-topped island, a new stainless steel refrigerator, a top-end stove with a convection oven, and ceramic tile on the floor.

Back upstairs, I started water running in the big claw-foot bathtub. I would probably turn the water black, but I could rinse with the shower and clean out the tub. If he was coming home after three in the morning, I would be able to soak until the water got cold, then refill it and wash. I couldn't remember the last time I had the luxury of soaking in a large tub.

The shelf above the tub held everything a girl could possibly want. I remembered the sad expression on his face when he told me his sister died. If she was anything like him, I bet I would have liked her. And she probably would have been horrified by me. I poured a capful of lavender bath oil in the water, and let the tub fill while I sipped my orange juice.

When the tub was full, I removed the knife hanging around my neck and put it next to the tub. Then I slid into the water and realized why that day seemed so strange. Obviously, I had died and gone to heaven. None of this could possibly be real. Ex-Marines with hearts of gold only happen in fairy tales, especially handsome, gentle ex-Marines, and fairy tales don't happen in the real world.

It took two tubs to soak off the grime, and I washed my hair four times before my scalp felt clean. My hair was so filthy that the shampoo didn't even lather properly the first time.

A long thin case on the top of the dresser drew my attention. I opened it and found a flute. McGarrity said he played guitar and his brother had a band. Evidently, they were a musical family. He recognized the Segovia number I played at the bar, which surprised me.

Looking in the dresser, I found a pair of cotton panties that fit me and a large t-shirt. Mary probably swiped it from her brother. I checked in the closet, and just as he said, there were jeans in the back, as long as I didn't mind them being six inches too long. The tops, shirts and shells were a little loose. That figured. The bra in the dresser was far too large. I might have fit my head in one of the cups, but not my boob.

It didn't matter. I really didn't need a bra, anyway. I turned back the bed, turned out the light, and slipped between clean, crisp linen sheets. I said a quick prayer that this was all real and that I wouldn't wake up with a drug-fueled hangover in the morning, discovering I'd been dreaming.

CHAPTER 3
Jake

Jared's pickup wasn't at the house when I got home. I wasn't surprised. He had two or three girlfriends, who seemed happy to share their beds with him, and he rarely came home at night. I didn't give a damn where he slept as long as he opened the restaurant at eleven every morning.

Trying to be quiet, I let myself in. The house was silent, but I could see a light on in the laundry room. Going back there, I found the girl's clothes in the washer, still wet. Having thrown them in the dryer, I turned out the light and went into the kitchen.

I poured myself a shot of whiskey, downed it, and then went back to the foyer and took off my boots. When I went upstairs, I didn't see a light under the door of Mary's room. Being very quiet, I flipped on the hall light, turned the knob and peeked in. Cecily lay on her side, sleeping peacefully. Her face was clean and her hair was wrapped in a towel. It appeared that she found an old t-shirt of mine that Mary used to sleep in. Her right hand was outside the covers, resting on the other pillow. The knife she held gleamed in the faint light from the hallway.

I chuckled. The girl would have fit right in over in Afghanistan. Except for her size. She had been bowed by the weight of her backpack, which I estimated only weighed thirty-five pounds. A Marine would have considered that light enough to go swimming with. Even a woman Marine.

I closed the door and went to my room, where I dreamed of an angel with Cecily's face descending from the sky.

In the morning, I awoke to the sounds of someone trying to be quiet in the kitchen. The smell of fresh coffee and bacon frying told me that either Cecily was awake, or

Jared had undergone a miraculous transformation the night before. I put on some clothes and went downstairs.

Cecily had set the table for two. A coffee mug sat beside the stove, along with a large glass of orange juice. Bacon lined up like soldiers at attention on a plate. She was wearing a t-shirt that was many, many sizes too large for her. If she had anything at all under it, I couldn't tell, as it covered her to her knees.

A towel wrapped her head, and without the grime, her freshly-scrubbed face glowed. Being clean also showed just how thin she was. Her cheekbones were so prominent it gave her a slightly foreign, elven look, and her legs looked like sticks. To be fair, she was so fine boned that I doubted she had ever weighed very much.

The cat was bumping around her ankles, meowing.

She turned and took a couple of steps toward me before she realized I was standing there.

"Oh, you startled me," she said. "I was just going up to ask how you like your eggs."

"Over easy," I said.

She went back to the stove and broke eggs into the frying pan. "There's fresh coffee," she said. "I don't know how you like it."

"Black is fine," I said with a smile, and went to pour some in the cup sitting beside the coffee maker. "This is a pleasant surprise. I could smell it upstairs. If Jared was cooking, I figured I'd be seeing flying cows when I went outside."

She smiled at me, her face lighting up, and my heart almost stopped. "I was hungry. I hope you don't mind. You said it was okay to look in the fridge."

"I don't mind at all. Did you sleep well?"

"Yes. Thank you for putting my clothes in the dryer. I guess I forgot. What's the cat's name?"

I felt my face flush. Cecily looked at me expectantly.

When I didn't answer, she said, "Doesn't she have a name?" She reached down and scratched the cat's ears. "Are you one of Mr. McGarrity's strays? Why didn't he give you a name?"

"We call her the Slut-Kitty," I mumbled. "Jared named her that because she wants to be petted all the time and she doesn't care who pets her."

Cecily laughed, then knelt down and scratched the cat's ears again. "You probably had a hard life before you came here, didn't you?" she said to the cat. "Well, there's no shame in being a slut. That's just a label foolish men and dried-up old ladies use for friendly girls. You and I will get along fine."

She slid a couple of eggs onto a plate, accompanied by several slices of bacon, and pulled a slice of toast out of the toaster. "Here, go sit down and eat before it gets cold."

She cooked her own eggs, scrambled with some cheese, and joined me. Looking at me with a pair of eyes that seemed too large for her face, she said, "I wasn't sure last night if I'd wake up this morning and find that yesterday was just a dream. I didn't know there were cowboy angels. Or that any angels cared about me. Thank you, Mr. McGarrity."

"Cecily," I said, "you make me very uncomfortable when you thank me every ten minutes. And people who know me would laugh at the idea of me being an angel. You needed a helping hand, and it hasn't hurt me any to give it to you."

"Those people don't know you very well," she said. "Everyone talks about Christian charity, but there aren't very many people who practice it. I'm more used to people calling me names when I'm standing on the side of the road than having them give me a ride."

That gave me an opening. "Where are you going?"

"California. I thought I might be able to find some work there."

"Playing music?"

"Yeah. It's the only thing I know how to do. I guess I could wait tables, but I'll try to get a music gig first."

"You've got that now," I said smiling.

She returned the smile. "Yes, I do, don't I? Thank you so ..." she trailed off as I held up my hand. "Oh, yeah, you're not comfortable with thanks, are you?" With a mischievous grin, she said, "Well, damn you very much, Mr. McGarrity, for giving me a job. Is that better?" She picked up our plates, and laughing, took them to the sink.

Her laughter was like silver bells. She quickly washed the dishes, ignoring the dishwasher, dried them and put them away.

She pulled the towel off her head, and bending forward, let her hair fall, gave it a shake, and then straightened. It fell down her back and over her shoulders in a cloud. Thick and at least a shade lighter now that it was clean, it was an astounding amount of hair

"Do you mind if I use your sister's brush?" she asked.

"No. You can have it, if you like."

She gave me another one of those smiles that turned my knees to jelly. "Damn you, Mr. McGarrity." Chuckling as she left the kitchen, she said, "If there are other words you would prefer I use instead of *thank you*, let me know."

Her bare feet pounding on the stairs as she ran up them reminded me of Mary.

She came back down looking much better than she had the day before, but the image of an angel stopped at her neck. "Cecily, we need to get you some clothes. You can't perform looking like that."

She looked down at herself, and then raised her eyes to mine. "I know they're pretty bad. But I can't afford clothes right now. All the money I have is what you gave me last night."

"I'll advance you some pay," I said. "Come on."

I needed to check on the horses and feed them, and she trailed me out to the stable. The dogs came at a run when they heard us.

"Sit," I commanded, and they plopped their butts down and looked at me expectantly. Their curiosity had them glancing at Cecily, but mostly their attention was on my closed hands.

"Are you comfortable with dogs?" I asked.

"Sure. Can I pet them?"

I turned to her, blocking my hands from the dogs' sight. "Here," I said, holding out my hands with the two dog biscuits. "Offer them on your open palm if you value your fingers. Then you can pet them."

She smiled and took the biscuits. "Barney and Mari, right?"

The dogs minded their manners and didn't try to eat her hands along with their treats, then leaned against her legs as she scratched their ears.

Inside the stable, I introduced her to the horses. "This is Maggie. That's Bella over there, and the two duns are Lightning and Thunder."

"They're all yours?" she asked.

"Mine and Jared's. Have you ever ridden a horse?" I asked as I put oats in their buckets.

"I rode a pony at a fair, once," she answered.

"Would you like to learn?"

Her eyes got wide and she looked very closely at the horse I was feeding. "Is it hard? I know that people take riding lessons for years."

"No, not that hard. I'm not talking about teaching you to jump and do fancy stuff, but they need exercise. I enjoy just taking them out for a ride. There's a pond a couple of miles from here. Nice place for a picnic."

A smile blossomed on her face and her eyes lit up. "Really? Yeah, I think I would like that."

"Then get to know Maggie. She's the one you'll be riding. She's getting along in years, but she's still fit and a real sweetheart." I handed Cecily a carrot. She seemed almost shy as she approached Maggie and fed her the carrot, then reached up and scratched her ears.

After I finished my chores, we hopped in my truck and headed to town. She brought her guitar with her. I had the feeling she never let it out of her sight.

"Do you play any other instruments?" I asked as we drove.

"Pretty much anything with strings," she said. "Mandolin, violin and cello, along with guitar. I play a fairly good pedal steel, banjo, and bass, but not as well as guitar."

Violin and cello? "How about electric guitar?" I asked.

She shot me a look that said I was a bit simple minded. "I can play anything you can play on a guitar," she said. "Have you heard Eric Clapton's unplugged album?"

"Some folk and classical guitarists don't ever pick up an electric," I said in my defense.

"Kind of hard to lug an amp around when you're hitchhiking" she said. "And an electric is useless without a place to plug it in. The Martin can be played anywhere."

When we got to the mall, I jumped out of the truck and started to lock it. But she just sat there.

"Mr. McGarrity, when you offered me a gig last night, you said Wednesday through Sunday. Wednesday was yesterday."

Smiling, I said, "There will be one next week, too. I checked the calendar. The forecasters predict one every week until the end of the year. I haven't seen a calendar for next year, though."

She didn't smile. "Does that mean you're offering me a job to play every week?"

"Yes, Cecily. Every week. As long as you play the way you did last night, wear some decent clothes, and don't do anything that would make me fire you, you've got a job as long as you want it. I talked with Kathy, my assistant manager, last night. What you predicted would happen did. People stayed after dinner and ordered more drinks. It was my best Wednesday ever. If you want a job, you've got it."

"If you give me an advance, can I pay you over time? Like take twenty-five dollars out each night until I pay you back? This isn't going to be cheap. I need everything. I don't even own a bra. Can you afford five hundred dollars?"

I noticed there wasn't a bra when I loaded her clothes in the dryer. A surge of elation shot through me. At the rate she was suggesting, it would take her a month to pay me back. I wouldn't mind having her around that long. Not at all.

"There's something else," she said. "If I'm going to stay here for a while, I'll need to get an apartment. I'll have to borrow money against my pay to do that, too."

"It's just me in that big old house," I told her. "My brother theoretically lives there, but he's never home. I'll tell you what. Help with the housework, cook me breakfast, and we'll worry about an apartment sometime down the line."

She gave me one of those grins of hers. "Sort of like having a wife, without all the entanglements, huh?" Climbing out of the truck, she said, "If you want all the wifely benefits, though, you have to make breakfast sometimes, too. I may be cheap and easy, but a girl has to set some limits."

I stood there stunned as she walked away. Turning back, she said, "Are you coming?"

~~~

Chapter 4
Cecily

We walked out of the mall after three hours, laden down with shopping bags, and I had a wardrobe. I told the sales lady in the western store to burn my old clothes. My new cowboy boots pinched a little, but Jake said they would loosen up as they broke in. I also had a nice pair of flats, and a pair of three-inch pumps with stiletto heels.

I bought three pairs of boot-cut blue jeans, some western shirts, a few blouses, three dresses and two skirts. By shopping the sale racks, I'd managed to keep it under the five hundred I estimated, including two bras and a two-week supply of panties.

When I did my laundry the night before, I threw the panties in the trash. As yucky as the idea was of wearing another woman's panties, the idea of even touching the ones I took off was worse. So I'd taken some of Mary's. Not any of the sexy ones, just a few pairs of cotton ones, sticking them in my pack. They fit. She might have been taller than I was, but very slender.

I wasn't sure all the clothes would fit in my backpack, but I'd worry about that later. It had been so long since I had any decent clothes.

Help with the housework? I had never done housework in my life. But if that's what he wanted, I could learn. I'd learn calculus or cow roping if it kept me near him. I chided myself for falling in love so quickly, but I wanted someone to love me, and something deep inside me wanted it to be him. I hadn't felt safe in years. The past six weeks had been filled with terror. And suddenly, out of nowhere, this man made me feel safe. I would do anything to continue feeling that way.

I felt like a new woman when I walked into the bar. Kathy looked at me and I saw her eyes widen in surprise.

Jake went behind the bar and motioned her over to where I took a seat.

"Kathy, meet Cecily. She's agreed to play for dinner Wednesday through Sunday evenings, from six until eight. I told her we'd pay her a hundred dollars a night out of the till."

Kathy nodded, not looking surprised.

"It's only seventy-five," I said, "until I can pay Mr. McGarrity back for the clothes he bought me."

She smiled, and I relaxed. Women are often uncomfortable with me, and seeing as I'd walked in off the street the way I did, and gone home with her boss, I wouldn't blame her at all for not liking me. But she didn't seem to have a problem with all this.

"It's nice to meet you," she said, sticking out her hand for me to shake. "You have a beautiful voice. I really enjoyed listening to you last night. What's your last name, honey?"

"Uh, Buchanan."

"I'll send Tom out to change the sign," she said, walking away toward the kitchen.

I looked at Jake.

"If we have a great new act, there's no reason to keep it a secret."

One of the cooks came out of the back and headed out the door.

"You might want to go with him," Jake said, "and make sure he spells your name right."

I trailed Tom out the door and watched as he got a tall ladder from the side of the building and leaned it against the sign. Climbing up with a canvas pouch over his shoulder, he pulled red letters out of it and started adding another line to the sign. When he was finished, it said, 'Dinner music by Cecily Buchanan Wed-Sun eves'.

I stood there, reading it over and over again while Tom put the ladder away. So many emotions boiling around inside me. I wasn't sure if I wanted to cry, cheer, or be terrified. But the chances of anyone connecting Cecille Buchanan of Baltimore with Cecily Buchanan in Greeley, Colorado, were pretty small. There wasn't a warrant for my arrest, as far as I knew. I went back into the bar and had a hamburger with fries and a glass of wine.

I played until 8:30, and then gave way to a bunch of cowboys who started setting up their instruments. I hadn't realized they were the band. They took a table right in front of the stage about eight, and listened to me play while drinking beer. The best looking one approached me as I was putting my guitar away.

"Hi, I'm Jared McGarrity, Jake's brother," he said, sticking out his hand.

I shook it. "Cecily Buchanan."

"My brother has some strange ideas sometimes," Jared said. "But he hit gold this time. Welcome aboard, Cecily. I haven't heard anyone play like that in a long, long time. We should be doing the intro for you."

I felt my face warm a bit. "Thank you. I'm really looking forward to hearing you play. Mr. McGarrity told me about your band. He's pretty proud of you."

"Mr. McGarrity? You mean Jake? Proud of me?" He shot a look over his shoulder at Jake, standing behind the bar watching us. "That's kind of nice to hear. All he ever tells me is that I'm a knucklehead."

Jared and his band took the stage while I put my guitar out of the way behind the bar and sat down. Jake poured me a glass of wine.

"Mr. McGarrity," I started, but he held up his hand.

"Please, call me Jake. You're making me feel old, and people around here are teasing me about you being so formal."

"I'm sorry. I certainly don't think you're old," I said, running my eyes over his body, his strong, handsome face. "I was just trying to be respectful. You are my boss, after all. What did you think? Was the set I did okay?"

"Cecily, you talked about angels this morning. I don't know what angel sent you here, but I'm glad he did. You are a rare talent. What in the hell are you doing here?"

I bit my lip. It was a reasonable question, and I didn't want to lie to him. "Is it okay if we don't talk about my past?" I asked. "I don't want to think about yesterday. I feel as though I've stepped into a whole new world." I looked into his face. "Jake, can you just accept that some really bad decisions brought me to your door, and let us move on from there?"

He stared at me for what seemed the longest time, then nodded. "Yes, we can do that. If you ever want to talk, I'll be glad to listen. But I can understand. I give people the same kind of answer when they ask me about my time in the Marines."

He reached out, squeezed my hand, and then drifted away to help a customer.

Maybe, I thought, but I'll bet what he says doesn't include the phrase 'bad decisions'. I was the queen of bad decisions. It would be nice to get my crazy life under control. I watched him while he worked. I had finally met a nice guy, and I wondered if I was smart enough to hang on to him. We only met the night before, but when he looked at me, his eyes said that he was interested. Interested didn't begin to describe the way I felt about him.

When the band took their first break, Jared came and sat next to me at the bar. "Jake says you play electric, too."

"Yeah. I can play just about anything with strings." That wasn't a boast.

"Would you like to play a few songs with us? I have an extra guitar."

"I don't know that many country songs," I said. "But listening to you, I was thinking about some songs I'd like to hear. Do you guys know any Willie or Emmylou?"

"Wow! Yeah, with your voice, we could do some Emmylou stuff."

"Is your other guitar tuned the same?" I asked.

"No. Want to go take care of that?"

We went up on stage and he handed me a white Fender Stratocaster, a Jimi Hendrix guitar. Jared had been playing a hollow-body Gibson most of the evening, but switched for a few songs.

Strapping on the Strat, I strummed it to hear how it was tuned. And then one of my imps seized control. I launched into *Purple Haze*, running the entire introductory riff. When I stopped and looked around, everyone in the bar was staring at me.

Stepping to the mic, I said, "Sorry. I'm not used to driving a guitar this powerful. It just sorta got away from me."

Everyone laughed.

We got me in tune with the rest of the band, and when the other members came back from their break, Jared introduced me.

"We have a special treat tonight, a psychedelic rocker from the East Coast." That got a laugh. "Those of you who happened to catch her playing here during dinner last night or tonight know what a special talent she is, and she's graciously agreed to sing a couple of songs with us. Please welcome Miss Cecily Buchanan."

Their band was tight and I liked playing with them. Jared was an excellent lead guitarist, and their pedal steel player was pretty good. The bassist and drummer were also good musicians. The rhythm guitarist was adequate, but had a nice voice. We played half a dozen Emmylou Harris songs, including *Luxury Liner, Quarter Moon in a Ten Cent Town, Roses in the Snow, Boston to Birmingham, Even Cowgirls Get the Blues,* and I sang a duet of *Hello Stranger* with Jared.

I've never been shy on stage, and the applause and cheers as I put the guitar down and stepped off the bandstand felt as good as if I'd been playing Carnegie Hall. It's better than food. I drank it all in shamelessly. For the first time in years, I felt whole, like myself. I remembered that I used to live for that feeling. How had I gone so far astray? This was so much better than any drug.

Jake came out from behind the bar and I skipped toward him. I threw my arms around his waist and gave him a hug. He hugged me back, in a friendly sort of way. His large strong hands on my back felt good. He didn't try to pull me into him, and for some reason, it didn't make me feel uncomfortable.

"Damn, Cecily, you're incredible," he said.

I looked up in his face. He was smiling and happy for me. Filled with approval. My heart seemed so full I thought it might burst. Where had this man been? Why hadn't I run into him two years ago? Someone who seemed genuinely happy when I succeeded, instead of jealous?

I pulled his face down to mine and kissed him on the lips. "You can't imagine how happy you've made me, and I've barely known you a day," I said.

When she wasn't busy, Kathy came over to where I was sitting at the bar watching Jared's band. We chatted a bit, and I could tell she was curious about me, but she didn't push.

"I've never known a Marine before," I said at one point. "I always imagined them as being very serious and stoic. Jake isn't that way at all."

She cocked her head and gave me a funny look. "Most people see him exactly that way," she said. "I worked for his parents, so I've known him since he was a kid. Jake was always different. When he graduated high school, he received a full-ride scholarship to play football, and a much smaller scholarship to study music at a liberal arts college back east. No one who really knew him was surprised when he chose music."

"Jake played football?" I asked. He was certainly built, but seemed a bit small, being barely six-feet tall.

"He was an all-state running back," Kathy said. "Fast, quick and shifty, but he ran with power."

"That's the guy who carries the ball?" I knew as much about football as I did about building rockets. I had seen it on TV a couple of times but never paid any attention to it.

She chuckled. "Yes, that's the guy who carries the ball."

"But Kathy, you still haven't answered my question. You said most people think he's stoic and reserved. He's not that way at all."

"What I was trying to explain," she said, "is that he has a sensitive side. He's always been more interested in music and art than most people, at least around here. I think you bring that out. If you don't see him as the hard-ass Marine, it's because he's showing you that other side of him. Or maybe the side most people see isn't there when he's with you."

"Oh." I didn't quite know what to say to that.

"Cecily," Kathy said, "I don't want to speak out of turn, but I've never seen Jake look at a woman the way he looks at you. I hope you appreciate the kindness he's shown you, and that you won't take advantage of him."

In his truck on the way home, he said, "I was a music major in college. Unfortunately, I suffered some nerve damage to my left hand in the service. I can still chord a guitar, but I don't have the fine control to play the violin any more, or to get real fancy on the guitar. But I can tell when someone is classically trained. Your voice isn't just a happy accident. It's opera quality."

Suddenly scared, I looked over at him. "Jake, please."

"I'm not going to ask you about your past, Cecily. But you said you can play anything with strings. Does that include the lute, Celtic harp and the sitar?"

I bit my lip and didn't answer him. His question really scared me. Was the list he mentioned just an accident?

"Watching you on that stage tonight," Jake continued, "you turned my brother's band into a supporting cast without any effort at all. You were the star. You've played a lot bigger venues than bars, haven't you?"

"Jake, don't make me lie to you. Please?" Oh, God. This wasn't going well at all. Although the tone of his voice was kind, he was asking all the wrong questions.

"Okay." His voice mellowed, and I breathed easy when I heard him backing off. "I don't know how you got here, or what you're running from, and it's none of my business. But, honey, a blind man could see that you stick out like a bottle of champagne at a college keg party."

He didn't say anything else. I was close to panic. Had I been stupid, performing in public? But I had to eat, and music was the only marketable skill I had. Maybe I should run again, get away before anyone discovered who I was, where I was. But I really couldn't do that. I owed Jake for the clothes he'd bought me. For feeding me last night. For believing in me just because I asked him to. Hell, he was taking me home, putting me in a soft, warm bed, and not even expecting to share it.

I decided he really was an angel, and as long as I stayed with him, everything would be all right. I just had to believe that. All of my other options led back to the madness.

I hadn't dreamed the night before. I guess I was too exhausted. But the dreams came that night. Not the worst ones, but I was standing on a stage with spotlights blinding me, and then out of the lights came a face, and he was reaching for me. I struggled to get away, but no matter how hard I ran, he was always there when I turned to look.

~~~

Chapter 5
Jake

It had been two weeks since Cecily came to live with me. I could see her cheeks starting to fill out from regular meals. The seat of her jeans, too. She told me when we bought her clothes that they were the size she wore, and assured me that they really weren't too big. She obviously hadn't been on the streets so long that she didn't remember her life before.

She had a bright, sunny attitude, a quick smile, and an infectious enthusiasm that endeared her to everyone who met her. The shell-shocked look I saw in her eyes that first day had faded, but the enigma of her past remained.

After she kissed me that night, I made sure to keep a safe distance from her. No more spontaneous hugs. Not that I didn't want her in my arms, but it would be far too easy to fall for her. The way she smelled and the feel of her lips caused an immediate reaction south of my belt. I couldn't remember a woman affecting me that strongly, not even my first love.

I got up before she did one morning and started to make breakfast. The next thing I heard was her pounding down the stairs.

"You're not supposed to be doing that," she said. "That's my job. Unless you've decided to change our deal. Have you?"

Damn, she looked hopeful. I took my coffee and backed out of the kitchen, and watched her face fall.

We quickly fell into a comfortable routine. Having her in the house felt natural. I think she was trying to hide that she didn't know how to cook or keep house. I walked into the living room one day and she was reading the label on a can of furniture polish, her brow furrowed in concentration. I realized she was trying to figure out how to use it.

My mom's cookbooks appeared on a shelf in the kitchen. She would pull one out, then look through the freezer, refrigerator and cabinets checking to see if we had all the ingredients to make a recipe she had chosen. When the recipe in question was beef stew, it was hard to ignore her checking the book every fifteen minutes to make sure she did everything correctly. I found her in the kitchen at the bar several times, mostly just watching, but also questioning the cooks on how to do something or why they did something, or even, "What is that spoon with all the holes in it for?"

It seemed a bit strange that a girl who had never learned anything domestic would suddenly become Miss Suzy Homemaker. I wondered if she was trying to put on an act. After watching her, both at home and at the bar, I decided it was something very different.

She wanted to please people, to make them like her. She was almost desperate to please, like a dog that had been abused. If anyone spoke harshly, she flinched, even though it wasn't directed at her. And it never was. Everyone loved her. She watched me constantly, gauging my reaction to everything she said. As I became aware of her behavior, I noticed she did the same thing with almost everyone.

I asked Kathy, trying to make it sound casual, what she thought of Cecily. In Kathy's typical no-nonsense manner, she said, "Someone in that girl's past deserves to be horse whipped. She's been treated very badly. I don't know if it was her parents, or a boyfriend. She treats any kind word like she did her food the day she walked in here. Like it's precious."

Occasionally, Cecily teased me about not wanting to sleep with her. But I could tell she had been in situations where she had grown used to giving men her body to survive. That's not what I wanted, nor did I want her to sleep with me out of gratitude. Hell, I couldn't decide if I wanted her to sleep with me at all, but I ached every morning when I saw her at breakfast. I wanted to touch her, to hold her, but I kept telling myself it wasn't the right thing to do.

I had to wonder exactly what she was hiding. Was it only bad experiences, or something more? A drunk tried to hit on her one night, and she reacted as if he was assaulting her. He never touched her, or even came within three feet of her, but she backed away from him, her hand going to the leather thong around her neck, and practically ran in the other direction. Another night, when a sheriff's deputy walked in the bar, I could have sworn her expression was one of pure terror. She quickly turned and headed for the ladies' room and didn't come out until he left.

I took her out to the garage one day and showed her my mom's car. The dogs followed us. They minded her as well as they did me, and they loved her. She would run with them, play tug-of-war, and scratch their ears and bellies until they had doggie orgasms. I noticed that the box of treats seemed to be emptier than I remembered. I asked her if she grew up with dogs, and she told me her mother had a toy poodle. It was the only time she answered any of my questions about her past.

Pointing to the car, I said, "It's just sitting there, Cecily. I can probably get it running again in a day or two. It needs an oil change, tune up, and a good checkup. It was running fine when Mom last drove it. Would you like to use it?"

"I don't know how to drive, Jake. I don't have a driver's license. Thanks for the offer, though." She stood looking at the car, and then she said, "How long ago did your mom die?"

I hated to think of that day, but it wasn't as though it was a big dark secret. Everyone knew what had happened.

"Three years ago. I was in Afghanistan, and Jared was starting his master's degree at the university in Boulder. My dad was a pilot, and he, Mom and Mary took off to fly to Aspen for the weekend. The plane went down in the mountains. It took them a few days to reach the wreckage, and it was too late."

I took a deep breath. The pain was still very sharp.

"The Marines let me out early, before my tour was up. Jared dropped out of school. We came home, sold off all the cattle and most of the horses, and took over the bar. Neither of us wanted to be a rancher. I guess we would have stayed home if that were the case. Mary loved it, though. Dad figured that maybe she'd marry a man who wanted to ranch and they'd keep the place going."

"How old was Mary?" Cecily's voice was almost a whisper.

"Nineteen. I think I miss her most of all. You always expect your parents to go during your lifetime, but she had her whole life ahead of her."

"The same age I am," Cecily said. "Three years ago, I was nineteen. She'd be twenty-two now. I'm so sorry, Jake."

I had thought Cecily might be even younger than that. But she had the same enthusiasm for life as Mary. Neither of them ever walked up or down the stairs. It always sounded as though they were in a race.

It helped to think of her as Mary's age. Mary was only thirteen when I shipped overseas the first time. A little girl. She had been eighteen the last time I saw her, at her high school graduation, so proud of her new smile with her braces off. The problem was that Cecily didn't look like a little girl. She looked like someone I wanted to undress.

But the problem of transportation remained. The ranch was twenty miles out in the country. Someone had to take her out there, or take her into town. I was dragging her around with me on all my errands, even to get a haircut.

"I can teach you to drive. It's not hard," I said.

Shaking her head, she said, "I really don't want to. I guess it's kind of a pain for you, though. As soon as I can get some money together, I'll get an apartment in town."

"Even in town, Greeley isn't New York. You need a car to get around. Don't you get tired of having to go everywhere with me? It can't be fun waiting for me all the time."

"I don't mind," she said. "I like being with you. But if you want to go someplace and don't want to take me, I understand. Just leave me here, or at the bar, or dump me at a coffee shop or something. If I can get to a main road, I can always get to the bar on time to sing. It must feel sometimes as if you're married, without any of the benefits. I'm sorry."

So was I. There was no doubt in my mind that I could have the benefits any time I asked. But it did feel good to hear her say she enjoyed being with me. It felt very good. Unfortunately, I had a feeling as to how she would get to the bar if Jared or I didn't take her. I had no intention of putting her in a position where she felt she needed to hitchhike.

And God help me, every time she mentioned getting an apartment, it felt like a knife through my heart. A wee bit fickle there, Jake? Want to eat your cake and have it too? We had only known each other a month, but I was convinced at times that if I asked her to marry me, she would only ask, how soon can we do it? My problem was that I caught myself daydreaming about a future with her. I hadn't felt lonely before she showed up.

If only I could get over the feeling that she was attracted to me because I was the only man who ever treated her like a human being. The way she looked at me sometimes was embarrassing. I'd seen that same look on the face of a teenaged girl meeting her rock star idol, and on the face of a nun praying to a crucifix. I was sure I was reading more into it than it deserved. Surely, it was impossible for me to be an object of worship. And the fact that I could even think that made me feel ashamed of myself.

It wasn't just my imagination that she was interested in crawling into my bed. I took her out riding, and it was obvious from the beginning that she had no idea how to ride a horse. But she liked it and was willing to work at it. The first day, we rode down by the creek. I took it easy, and Lightning wasn't too happy about it. Maggie, however, was a perfect lady, until we got close to the creek and she could smell the water.

Lightning broke into a trot, and Maggie followed him. I looked back and saw Cecily bouncing around in the saddle like a sack of flour. I winced. When we reached the water, cool and lined by willows on both sides, she was flushed and laughing.

"I need to teach you how to post," I said. "There's a way to ride a trotting horse that doesn't bounce you around like that."

"Oh, I don't mind," she said. Then she giggled. "Now I understand why girls like horses so much." She leaned down and patted Maggie's neck. "I never expected that I'd get my first orgasm at the Top Hat Ranch from another girl."

She gave me a pointed look, and I felt my own face flush.

On our way back to the house, I broached a topic that had been on my mind. "Would you be interested in playing more?" I asked. "Kathy and Jared and I have been talking, and one idea we've considered is having you start on Thursday and Friday at five. We've noticed people coming in after work just to have a drink and hear you sing."

It would be a long pull for a performer. As it was, I felt guilty. She was supposed to sing from six to eight, but she often played until eight-thirty, and as late as nine on the weeknights. People would keep asking for one more song, and she always obliged them. And sometimes, especially when Jared played, she'd get up and sing with the band. It seemed she never got tired of being on that stage.

"I could pay you another fifty a night on those nights."

"Sure," she said, her face lighting up. "I like to play."

I gave her an old hat of my Dad's to use for her tips. Kathy checked it a couple of times, and said on weekends Cecily was making as much on tips as we were paying her.

One night, an old girlfriend of mine came into the bar. Jeri and I had been a hot item, and we'd given our virginity to each other. Even after we went away to college in different states, we still got together when we came home for holidays. But six years away playing soldier was a bit too much, and she had gotten married. And divorced. Since I came back, we had gotten together a few times, but it just didn't seem right to me. I didn't love her anymore, and as good as the sex was, Jeri wanted more than I could give her.

Jeri was physically almost the opposite of Cecily, tall and busty with dark hair and eyes, she drew stares everywhere she went. Cecily tended to fade into the background unless she was playing, and I think she did it on purpose. Jeri was an extrovert, almost to the point of being an exhibitionist.

She came into the bar right after Cecily finished playing. I was on the floor, taking a tray of drinks to one of the waitress's tables. As per usual when Cecily was playing, the place was packed. Jeri walked up to me, threw her arms around me, and gave me a kiss.

"Damn, I swear you get better looking every day," Jeri said. "How the hell have you been doing?"

I laughed. "My mother warned me about women like you."

"No she didn't," Jeri said, "she warned you about *me*. There aren't any other women like me, only pale imitations."

Wrapping her arm around my waist and laying her head against my shoulder, she walked with me back to the bar. "I hear you got a new girlfriend," she said. "I'm devastated. You should at least give me a chance to arm wrestle her for you, or something."

Cecily swiveled toward us. "That's probably me," she said with a smile. "But I'm not his girlfriend. I just want to be."

I cringed.

Jeri laughed and walked over to her, extending her hand. "Me, too. I'm Jeri."

Cecily shook her hand, and Jeri sat next to her at the bar.

A large hand fell on my shoulder. "You are so screwed," Jared said in my ear. "What in the world were you thinking letting Jeri in here?"

"I couldn't get to the door fast enough to lock it when I saw her coming across the parking lot," I said.

"I'd consider whether you should find somewhere else for Cecily to be. You don't want Jeri sinking her claws into her. If Jeri decides to get nasty, I don't think Cecily can stand up to her."

Remembering Cecily sleeping with that damned knife clutched in her hand, I said, "Don't sell Cecily short. I have a suspicion her claws are bigger than you think. Jared, if anyone ever gets physical with her, step in quickly, but do it carefully. And if you ever decide to spend a night at home, be careful. The girl sleeps with a big-ass knife in her hand."

He gave me a shocked look.

"As a matter of fact, I think she's wearing it right now, on a thong around her neck."

"You're kidding me."

"No, I'm not. Have you noticed that she never wears low-cut dresses or anything without a collar? When she's asleep, treat her like a combat vet. I don't know where she's been, but wherever it was, she didn't feel safe."

He watched the two women chatting as if they were old friends.

"So instead of the cougar and the lamb ..."

"I think you're looking at the cougar and the lynx. I may be wrong. Cecily might crumple in a confrontation, but I don't think so. She's smart, and although we haven't seen it, I have a feeling she could shred someone with her tongue."

I watched Jeri and Cecily. They sat there and talked almost all night. When Jeri got ready to leave, she walked over to me, put her arms around my neck, and kissed me again.

"You know, Jake, I think you're a fool for not wanting me in your bed tonight. I'm really not as crazy as you think I am."

Stepping away from me, she said, "But you're not only a fool, but a damned fool and a mean one for keeping that little girl around and not giving her what she wants. Either send her packing, or tell her you love her. Don't torture her. The Jake I know would never be as cruel as you're being to her."

Then she walked out and didn't look back.

I remembered that conversation with Jared a couple of weeks later when a drunk started heckling Cecily on stage. I was hurrying toward him when she stopped singing.

"Oh, my," she said. "You must be the guy people have been telling me about. Are you the guy who fell in the pig trough and got his balls chewed off? Is that why you want to pick on a girl?"

The audience laughed him out of the bar. I only had to steer a little bit.

"I'm terribly sorry about that," I heard Cecily say as I shoved the drunk out of the door. "Some people can't hold their liquor very well. And you know what happens then, don't you? They open their mouths and let everyone know how smart they are. It's usually a disappointment. Does anyone have a request?"

~~~

CHAPTER 6
Cecily

I had a conversation with one of Jared's girlfriends at the bar one night. Jake told me that Jared and Karen had been on and off for about two years. I went to get a glass of fruit juice on my break and sat down next to her at the bar. Kathy took my order and brought my juice.

"How's it going?" I asked Karen. She looked kind of down.

"Hell, Cecily, I don't know."

"What's the matter?" I was still somewhat surprised that women here liked me. I never had girlfriends, but Jeri, Karen, and a couple of other regulars at the bar, along with Kathy and the waitresses, seemed to accept me and treat me like I belonged in Greeley, Colorado. I never felt that people treated me like an outsider.

"I'm just getting tired of Jared treating me like an afterthought," she said. "I know he's allergic to commitment, but sometimes, I think I should stop being a fool and move on."

"Do you love him?" To me, the question wasn't a formality. A woman might stay with a man for a lot of reasons.

"Yeah, I do. I know I'm a damned fool, because he obviously isn't in love with me, but every time I break it off, I end up running back to him."

I asked what to me was the most important question, and I watched her face carefully, "How does he treat you?"

"He treats me like a queen when he's with me. He never forgets my birthday. Even when I broke up with him, he still bought me a Christmas present. But he's not with me enough, and every time I turn around, he's screwing someone else. I'm just tired of it."

"Well, I guess that's something you have to decide," I said. "For me, I'd rather have a man who treats me well and makes me feel loved one day a week, than one who abuses me seven days a week."

I wasn't sure what I said wrong, but both Karen and Kathy looked a bit shocked.

"You wouldn't mind being part of a harem?" she asked. "How would you feel if Jake had a harem of women?"

"I wouldn't care," I said, "as long as I was part of the harem."

I got up to go back to the stage and play my next set.

"Well, you don't have to worry about that with Jake," Karen said. "He's the kind of man who doesn't screw around. All he wants is one special girl."

My breath hitched in my throat. Maybe that was the problem. I just wasn't that girl. "You think so?"

There must have been something in my voice, because Karen shot me a look. "Of course," she said. "Everyone knows he's head over heels about you."

It was suddenly hard to breathe, and my eyes filled to where I couldn't see very well. "Everyone except me," I managed to say, and then fled to the restroom.

I leaned against the wall next to the sink, holding my stomach and sobbing. I thought I had it so well together, but I couldn't deny how much it hurt.

Kathy came in and stood in front of me. "Are you okay?" she asked. "What did Karen say?"

"She didn't say anything. She was just complaining about Jared," I said, trying to get myself together. I pushed off from the wall and started drying my eyes with a paper towel.

"I told her that I would rather have a man who treated me like a queen one day a week than a man who was around all the time and treated me badly."

"Has Jake been treating you badly?" Kathy asked, and I could hear the incredulity in her voice.

The question shocked me. "Jake? Of course not. He doesn't treat me any way at all. He treats me like a little sister. I think I'm sort of a substitute for Mary."

"Ahh," was all Kathy said.

I washed my face, dried it, and went back out to play my set. But I started thinking that I should change my situation. It had been a very long time since I wanted a man to touch me, and now that I did, he wouldn't.

Jake was preparing the bar for Fourth of July, and had been running ragged all week. I needed to go to the store for tampons before going to work, and Jake picked me up late. Since then, I had been thinking about talking to him.

A month before, I finally pulled the money together to set up an appointment with a gynecologist. Everything checked out okay, and the results of all the tests were negative, for which I heaved a huge sigh of relief.

We were eating breakfast one morning when I decided I had to say something. When I got up that morning, I felt a bit depressed. I couldn't talk to him, or tell him anything about myself. Usually I didn't think about that too much, but that morning it hit me hard. He obviously didn't feel what I did.

"Jake, I've saved enough to get an apartment in town," I started, watching his face closely. "Don't you think it would be better for me to look now, before all the university students come back to town?"

"You don't need to move out," he said. "Save your money."

"Well, I think it would be best."

He finally looked at me. "Why?"

"I really appreciate everything you've done for me. Honestly, I believe you saved my life. I've been low before, but I was never as close to giving up as I was that day. I really wondered if I would lie down in a ditch some night and never wake up. But it's not fair to you. You have your life, and instead of being able to live it the way you want, it all revolves around me. Pick me up from here to go to work. Bring me back. Take me to the doctor or the store. I think I should let you have some time to yourself."

"Renting an apartment will be expensive," he said.

"I have over three thousand dollars saved. There's an apartment complex only a mile from work where I can get an efficiency for four hundred a month. I have to pay first and last and a two hundred dollar deposit, but I've got the money. And there's a bus that runs from there right by the bar."

"You don't have to move out, Cecily. I like having you here. The place would feel lonely without you."

Now came the hardest part. The part I really didn't want to say.

"Jake, I haven't been sleeping well. It's hard. You're right down the hall, and I want to be with you, and I can't. I need to move. It will be much easier to be friends if we have some space. But I don't think I can do this anymore. It just aches to see you every morning and not be able to touch you."

I rehearsed the speech to him over and over, and I still didn't say it the way I meant to. That last sentence wasn't anything I ever planned to say, it just slipped out.

"You think you have to move out so we can be friends?" he said carefully.

He could be so frustrating sometimes. I felt tears start to spill from my eyes. In all the scenarios I had run through my head about this talk, none included me crying. I pushed away from the table and stood.

"Don't you understand?" I practically screamed at him. "I don't want to be friends. I want you to love me the way I love you."

Oh, shit. The shock in his face mirrored what I was feeling. Dear God, what was wrong with me? I wheeled about and ran up the stairs. When I reached Mary's room, I slammed the door behind me and fell on the bed.

Wiping the tears from my face, I cursed myself as an idiot. Of all the things I could have said, I couldn't have created a bigger disaster. I've lost him for sure, I thought. Maybe I still had a chance before, but now it's all over. I may have been dumb about men, but I knew the easiest way to scare them was to talk about love or marriage. And no man wants to deal with a hysterical, crying female. He probably thinks I'm trying to manipulate him.

I heard the door open.

"Go away. I don't want you to see me like this. I'm pathetic," I said.

He came over and sat on the bed. Pulling me up into a sitting position, he wrapped his arms around me and pulled me to him. I knew he was just trying to be kind, but it felt so good to lay my head against his chest. I was pathetic. I grasped at every kindness like it was a lifeline. I didn't blame him for not wanting to get entangled with me. Everything I touched turned into a horrible mess.

"Cecily, I'm sorry," he said. "I'm such a fool. I kept telling myself that it wouldn't be fair to you. That I would just be taking advantage of your gratitude. I want you so bad. I love you, and so I tried to keep you away."

I thought I understood the words he was saying, but I couldn't make sense of them. My head was so screwed up that I was twisting what he said. He was so kind. I was taking advantage of him. I knew it. How could I do that to someone who loved me?

What? I put my hands on his chest and pushed away from him. "What did you say?"

"I said I love you, and I'm sorry I've been hurting you."

I stared at him, blinking stupidly. "You love me?"

"Yes. I've been in love with you almost since the first night. I just didn't want to take advantage of you. You were so damaged, so alone."

I reached up and took his face between my hands, and kissed him. Kissed him and kissed him. Parting his lips with my tongue, I tried to crawl inside him. I pulled him down on the bed, on top of me.

"If you love me, then show me," I whispered into his mouth. "I've lain here night after night, dreaming of you making love to me. Make that dream come true."

"Are you sure?" he asked.

"I'm going to hit you. Shut up and kiss me."

I had dreamed of having his hands on me, but the reality was so much better. His rough-calloused hands ignited sparks everywhere he touched me. He was gentle, taking it slow, which was the exact opposite of my agenda. I pushed him away, and taking his shirt in my hands, frantically pulled it apart. Thank God for cowboy shirts with snaps instead of buttons.

His chest was broad and muscular with dark hair like a soft carpet. I reached back and unhooked my dress, then leaned forward.

"Unzip me," I said.

He pulled the zipper all the way down and I let it slide over my shoulders. Pressing my bare breasts against him felt so good. I held him and reveled in feeling his skin next to mine. But that wasn't all I wanted. I pushed away from him again and started unfastening his belt. That done, I unzipped his pants.

"Get undressed," I said, pushing my dress and panties over my hips, then tossing them to the floor. He was too slow, and I pushed him over on his back. Standing over him on the bed, I pulled his jeans over his feet and threw them to the side. My eyes feasted on his naked body, and then I dove into his arms.

My urgency increased. Kissing him while I wriggled around on top of him, I finally managed to straddle him. Sliding down over his stomach, I felt behind me and grasped his erection. Rising to my knees, I guided him into me and sank down until I had all of him in me.

"Oh, God," I moaned.

"Cecily, we need a condom," he said.

"No, we don't," I said. "That's why I went to the doctor. All my tests are clean and I got a new implant."

I rode him hard and fast until we both cried out as we reached our climax. Falling forward onto his chest, the sense of frantic urgency finally flowed out of me. He was so warm and soft and solid and comfortable. I nestled against him and purred.

We finally crawled out of bed in mid-afternoon. Taking a shower with him was every bit as wonderful as I'd imagined it would be. We washed each other, and then I washed my hair. It was still wet when we left for work.

Sitting beside him as we drove into work, I realized that I had actually made love for the first time, in the sense that I had sex with love. This was actually the first time I ever initiated sex. And it was the first time I ever had an orgasm with a man that didn't involve some sort of pain. I didn't know how closely I associated the two until I braced myself as I reached climax, expecting it to hurt as the price of the pleasure. But it didn't hurt at all. It was glorious.

I had to explain to Jake that I was okay. He was so concerned about the tears after I came. I told him they were tears of joy. And that was part of it, along with fear and relief. How could I tell him how sick I was? That I craved orgasms the way an addict craves drugs. That I loved the way men made me feel even when the men themselves repulsed and scared me. I couldn't count the number of times I had an orgasm, then went to the bathroom and threw up.

Every time I had sex before, I was raped. I had never thought of it that way before. Most of the time I hadn't said no, because I knew it was useless, and it might even cause the guy to hurt me more. But it was rape just the same. The drug in my drink the night I lost my virginity provided consent, but I was incapable of either refusing or consenting.

I sang love songs at the bar that night. Only love songs. Following him with my eyes while he worked, I sang to him. When I took a break, Kathy motioned me to come over to where she stood by the waitress station.

Looking me over, she said, "He finally came to his senses, didn't he?"

I bit my lip and stammered, then said, "I think so. I hope so."

"You're afraid he'll change his mind?" she asked.

I nodded.

"He won't," she said with conviction. "He's as mad about you as you are about him."

I climbed back onto the stage and sang more love songs.

That night, I slept in his bed. I took my knife off and left it on the dresser by the door of his room. But feeling warm and safe in his arms didn't stop the dreams.

It was one of the worst ones. Rough hands on my body, alcohol on his breath, his weight crushing me. Pain in my face where he hit me, pain in my groin as he forced himself inside me. The feeling of helplessness, terrified that he would hurt me even worse. The dream went on and on and I couldn't stop it. The dream ended with the horror that remained when he finally had stopped. I sat up in bed, gasping for air and shaking. That image stayed in my head all morning.

God, how could I let Jake love me when I was keeping such secrets? Didn't he deserve to know he was sleeping with a woman capable of such a thing?

~~~

Chapter 7
Jake

Life with Cecily in my bed was something I had never imagined. Oh, I fantasized about her, but the reality was very different. That first morning, when she stripped off her dress, I could only stare in awe. She was slender, but she wasn't skinny. Smooth firm flesh covered her frame, and the swell of her hips from that impossibly small waist took my breath away. I had thought she was wearing a bra, but her high, firm breasts didn't need one, and they were larger than I imagined.

She approached lovemaking the same way she approached performing on stage. It depended on her moods. One night she might want me to take it slow, drawing out our pleasure in a slow, sensual horizontal dance. The next night she might be playful, bouncing around, teasing, enthusiastic and wanting me to explore my fantasies, talking about hers. Still another night, she might be urgent, demanding, wanting me before we hardly got in the house.

To say that she was enthusiastic was like saying water is wet. She was in the mood all the time, and it took very little to bring her to climax. The first time I went down on her, I thought she would completely come apart.

She had no inhibitions, and nothing I ever suggested seemed to be out of bounds. I had never been with a woman who was so open about discussing our fantasies. But one of hers stopped me cold. She said that sometimes she wanted me to hurt her.

"And you enjoy that?" I asked, incredulously.

"Sometimes. Not most of the time. Not hurt hurt, really. I mean, I don't want you to hit me or anything. I just like it really rough sometimes." She looked away, then back to me. "I don't want you to get the wrong idea about what I'm going to say. You have to understand that I love you, and the only reason I would ask this is because I trust you. I know you would never really hurt me. Sometimes I want you to treat me really rough."

I ran this over in my mind. "Have you ever been raped?"

She was quiet for a long time, and then she whispered, "Yes. Before I met you. When I lived on the streets. When I was hitchhiking." She looked up at me with as open and vulnerable an expression as I had ever seen on a person. "I never knew what love was until I met you. I love the way you touch me."

There was a catch in her voice as she said, "No one was ever gentle with me before. Seeing the love in your face when we climax is the most incredible thing I could ever imagine."

She got up from the bed and stood looking out the window, tears running down her face. "Jake, I know I'm all messed up inside. Being raped was terrifying, horrible. But," her voice fell to where I could barely hear her, "sometimes I had orgasms when it happened. Really intense ones. I know that's wrong. Someone has to be really sick to do that. I don't want to be raped, but sometimes, I feel like I need to be punished. When I'm in a certain mood, I just want to be used as hard as you will let yourself use me. Can you do that for me occasionally?"

My God. 'Sometimes I had orgasms' she said. How many times had she been raped? Enough that some of the times were better than the other times. I thought of the knife. She still wore it around her neck. I never asked about it, and she never mentioned it. She always took it off when she entered our bedroom, and left it by the door.

I knew that she had dreams, nightmares. She didn't thrash around or scream or anything like that, but I could tell when she was having one. Her body would stiffen, and she would whimper. I interpreted the expressions on her face at those times as being those of terror or pain. I didn't know if I should wake her up, so I would just hold her, stroke her hair, and whisper over and over that I would take care of her and it would be all right. Sometimes it seemed to quiet her.

Jeri took Cecily over to Fort Collins and she found a violin in a pawnshop. It was only fair quality, but she said it was fine for her purposes. I had never heard her play violin before, and sat in awe listening as she played. I was considered good enough, perhaps, to apply to some orchestras before my injury. The difference between me as a third seat in a medium-level symphony and her, was the difference between Bob Dylan and Pavarotti.

Cursing myself for a fool, I crawled up in the attic and found my violin. When I gave it to her, she lit up like a lightning bug. But she kept the pawnshop instrument. She took it down to a music shop and had a pickup put in it. Then she tuned it to play bluegrass fiddle.

Shortly before Halloween, Jared brought the band's agent, David Thomas, to the bar to hear Cecily. The band was doing well. Dave was booking them all over the Rockies and putting them in some large venues. They were out of town most weekends now, and I could only get them into the Roadhouse on Thursdays, if at all.

Her performances varied widely, not the quality of the performance, but what she played and sang. It was her first performance after she got the fiddle and she played it a good deal, dancing around the stage to her own music. The band that night had a mandolin player, and she borrowed his instrument for a few songs. The variety put her in a lively mood, and she was much more animated than usual.

The mandolin player came over to the bar for a beer, and then leaned back and watched her. Shaking his head, he said, "Have you ever felt totally inadequate? How in the hell am I ever going to play that instrument again, knowing that it can sound like that?"

She also sang a couple of songs I'd never heard before. When she came over to get a drink on her break, I asked, "Are you singing your own compositions?"

"Yeah. Do you like them?" Her smile brightened.

"I like them a lot. I didn't know you wrote songs."

"Oh, yeah. I've got a couple of hundred I've written over the years. Do you want to hear some more?"

She didn't know the agent was there. He was sitting behind her, and I saw his ears perk up.

"Yes, do you think you could do a whole set of them to finish the night?"

Smiling, she said, "Anything for you," and kissed me.

She sang nine songs over the next hour. Ballads and love songs, and a song that would make a good dance number. At the end, she motioned me up to the stage, and using me as her foil, sang a hilarious song, making fun of herself by pointing out all of her supposed faults and foibles. It went on for thirty verses and included every supposed female fault that had ever been cataloged. The chorus at the end of each stanza was, "But the joke's on you, because you think I'm perfect. Oh, how wonderfully blind love is." She punctuated the end of the song by kissing me.

The audience loved it, laughing and joining her to sing the chorus.

She sang one encore, then turned the stage over to the band. Skipping across the bar, she threw herself into my arms, kissed me, and sang, "Oh, how wonderfully blind love is."

"Cecily, I'd like you to meet a friend of mine and Jared's. This is Dave Thomas. He's the agent who books Jared's band."

She stuck her tongue out at him and gave him a fake pout. "So, you're the one who's responsible for taking Jared away from us," she said. "We hardly ever get to see him anymore."

"Guilty as charged," Dave said. "But he's making a lot of money."

The fake pout disappeared into a bright smile. "Money's good!" she said. "I guess I can forgive you." She extended her hand and said, "It's nice to meet you, Mr. Thomas. Don't mind me, I'm in a mood tonight. I'll be more subdued when I come down off the performance."

"That was quite a performance," he said. "Are you interested in singing professionally?"

"I am a professional," she said proudly. "I get paid."

"What I mean," he said, "is I could book you into larger venues, ones with more exposure. I could put you in some big clubs in Denver and Boulder. I think you have the kind of talent to pitch to a record company."

Her demeanor changed entirely and the smile disappeared. She became very serious, and very distant.

"Thank you, Mr. Thomas. I appreciate your interest. I don't think I'm interested, however. I'm content just playing here at the Roadhouse."

She turned away and went to the restroom.

He looked at me. "Did I say something wrong?"

"No. I'm sorry, Dave," I said. "I don't know where that came from. I thought she'd be excited. You really think she has what it takes to make it?"

"All the way, Jake. You were right. She's a rare talent. The voice, the instrumental dexterity, and her stage presence are incredible. I think she can go as far as she wants to."

He shook his head. "I also think that she's too much for me. What I would do is take a small advisory fee and set her up with a big agent on the West Coast, someone with top-level connections. But we could start building her brand here in the Denver area while I can find the right situation for her."

"I'll talk to her, Dave. I never expected her to take that attitude. You saw her. She lights up on stage. She lives to perform."

That night, I said, "I'm sorry, Cecily. I thought you'd be excited by the chance to get some gigs. Dave thinks you have the talent to become a big star. He's not just blowing smoke. I've known him a long time, and he's a straight shooter. He knows the music business."

She put her arms around my neck and kissed me. "Thank you. It was very sweet, but I'm not interested. I'm happy here with you. All I want is to help you make the Roadhouse a success. Is that such a bad thing? To want to work with the man I love?"

Put that way, what could I say? She took me to bed, and all thoughts of anything but her went out of my head, as they always did.

Chapter 8
Cecily

I lay awake, listening to Jake breathing. I couldn't remember ever being so happy in my life. I had a man who loved me, who treated me like a princess. I was able to perform, and people liked what I did on stage. It was everything I ever wanted. No, I wasn't rich and famous. I wasn't traveling around the world, seeing my name in lights.

But those were the dreams of my younger self. Before I screwed up my life and discovered what was really important. Maybe I should have given Jake a different name instead of telling him my real one. I hadn't even thought about what it might mean to have my real name on that sign above the Roadhouse. But I also never expected to find love and kindness when I entered his bar. I didn't even know those things existed. Before I met Jake, they were only words.

All I could hope for is that Mr. Thomas went away and left me alone.

Of course, there was another issue that I was refusing to confront. If I loved Jake, and I did, how long could I go before telling him everything? He deserved the truth. I knew that I would be angry if I found out he had a big, horrendous secret that might explode in the middle of us, wrecking our lives and our plans for the future. I was so afraid he would send me away, or turn me in, if he knew my deepest secrets. I couldn't imagine how he would react if he knew how black my sins were. I knew he was going to heaven, and I was going to hell. My whole life with him was a lie.

He was talking about taking me to Hawaii for Christmas. But he would ask questions when I told him I couldn't get on an airplane. You needed identification to do that. I wondered how long it would be until he offered me a ring. I didn't care if he never did, as long as I had him. But he was an honorable man, and he would probably try to do what he thought was the honorable thing. In his world, two people married when they were in love.

As far as I was concerned, he could hide me under the bed and deny he even knew me, as long as he let me hold him and make love to him every night. I wasn't important, but he was my world. Would he throw me out if I told him the truth?

I asked Jake to drop me off downtown the next day, telling him I would take the bus to work. Going to the library, I entered a search for Cecille Buchanan. I found a lot of entries on the internet, but nothing in the past year and a half. The last flurry of activity was when I cancelled the tour. Probably the worst decision of my life.

I entered Eddie's name, and got a lot of hits. That also faded out, with nothing in the news during the past three months. In an earlier story, I found a reference to 'a mystery girl' that was connected to him, but not my name.

Relieved, I bought some ice cream and took the bus to the Roadhouse.

I managed to talk Jake and Jared into letting me clean out Mary's closet and her other belongings. I also cleared their parents' clothing and other personal items out of the attic. We donated it all to the church they attended when they were growing up.

Gradually, I turned the house into a home for Jake and me, not just a place to sleep. Jared only stayed there a couple of nights a week.

I had never done housework in my life. The vacuum cleaner was a complete mystery, but I found the instructions for it stuffed away in the 'junk drawer' and read them. Dusting, oiling the woodwork, cleaning the oven, all those sorts of things I had seen people do. I learned to do them, and because I was doing it for Jake, I loved it.

Cooking was another story. I knew how to make a simple breakfast and sandwiches, but I had never cooked a real meal. Since Jake bought groceries, and had a freezer full of meat, I assumed that he did. I found a couple of cookbooks in a drawer in the kitchen that were older than Jake, so I assumed they were his mother's. By following the directions exactly, and looking up every term I didn't understand, I managed to avoid any disasters.

One morning, when Jake went into town on business and to pick up some groceries, I stayed at home, cleaning and doing laundry. His CD collection was a marvel. Next to the Grateful Dead was Gustav Holst's *The Planets* symphony. And he had opera. I hadn't even heard an opera in two years before he brought me home.

Mozart's *Magic Flute* was playing at a volume where I could hear it throughout the house and I was singing along with it. Standing in the kitchen, I was singing 'Hell's vengeance boils in my heart', the Queen of the Night's aria from act three. It felt so good to stretch my voice and hit the notes of the soprano coloratura part, and I was lost in the music.

I took a breath to ready myself for the next lines, and realized he was standing at the edge of the kitchen, watching me. The woman on the CD sang on alone.

"Hi, I didn't hear you come in," I said.

"My God, Cecily," he said, "your voice is phenomenal."

"I listened to a lot of opera when I was growing up," I said, turning to continue wiping the top of the stove with the dishcloth I was holding.

"That's bullshit," he said, and I flinched. "I can understand you not wanting to tell me some parts of your life, but do you have to completely shut me out of all of it? No one can sing an aria like that unless they've been trained for it. Especially that one."

I bit my lip, turning to face him. "Jake, I don't know what to tell you. I never want to lie to you, so I don't tell you anything. It scares me, Jake. I'm so afraid that if you find out who I really am, how screwed up and damaged I am, that you won't love me anymore. Sometimes I want to tell you. Tell you everything. But I'm a coward. And I know that isn't fair to you, and it's tearing me apart."

He walked over and took me in his arms. "Nothing could stop me from loving you," he said.

My face hidden against his shoulder, I said, "You don't know how bad I am. I don't love me, how could I expect you to if you knew the truth?"

"How do I convince you to trust me?" he murmured into my hair.

"I trust you," I said. "You're the fool for trusting me."

I felt him stiffen. "Are you so bad that you need to be punished?" he asked.

"Yes, please," I whispered.

He picked me up and carried me across the room, slamming my back against the wall. Rough, careless hands pulled my shirt open, and tore my jeans off. With no foreplay or preparation, he penetrated me and pounded me, punishing me with his body. Feeling him driving hard and deep inside me as I rode the edge between pleasure and pain, it was as though he was driving a spear into all the evil and humiliation buried in my soul. When he climaxed, an orgasm slammed through me like a battering ram, and I screamed his name.

He withdrew, and held me in his arms, tears running down his cheeks. It was the first time he had been able to let go, to give me what I needed.

"Thank you," I whispered. "God, I love you, Jake."

"Is that really what you want me to do to you?" he asked.

"Yes. You need to punish me sometimes. When I hurt you. I don't mean to hurt you. I just can't help myself. You can't just let me hurt you and be silent. You need to punish me for it. You need to hurt me back and make things balance."

"God, Cecily, I don't know if I can do that again. I feel like ..."

"Shhh," I said, putting my fingers to his mouth. "Love has many ways of expression. You don't have to understand, Jake. Just know that you make me happy. And I'll try, I promise I'll try, to make you happy, too. I'll try to be better, Jake. I'm trying to learn to be good enough for you."

~~~

CHAPTER 9
Jake

Dave Thomas called me and asked if we could meet. I left Cecily at home cleaning the bathroom and singing along with an aria from one of my CDs. Since that day I came home and found her singing opera, she had opened up to admit that she'd had extensive classical training, both voice and instrumental. But she hadn't told me much more than that.

We met at the bar before my staff showed up to open for the day. He handed me three CDs. The name of the artist leaped out at me, Cecille Buchanan. One was 'Interpretations of Beethoven on the Celtic Harp', the next was 'Greatest Violin Solos', and the third was 'Operatic Arias'. The pictures in the liner notes confirmed that my Cecily and Cecille Buchanan were the same woman. I hadn't known her full name before, never thought to ask.

"Jake, I'm sorry if you think I'm sticking my nose in where it's not welcome. Something about the way Cecily acted that night didn't make sense. Just because I'm retired doesn't mean that I've lost my instincts."

I met Dave when I was still in the Marines. It was right after I came back from Afghanistan the last time. A young Marine in my company was murdered, and the FBI agent assigned to the case was Dave Thomas. He found the two men who were to blame.

We became friends, and when he retired the next year and moved to Colorado, we reconnected. In his youth, he was in a rock band that cut one album and had some momentary fame. When the band broke up, he went to college and then joined the FBI. In retirement, he wanted to get back into the music business and became a booking agent.

"Jake," he said, "the FBI and the Baltimore police are looking for your girl."

My head snapped up. A cold, numb feeling spread through my mind. "What did she do?"

"As far as I can find out, they aren't sure she did anything. The official line is that she's being sought as a material witness in a murder investigation." He shrugged. "That could be a smoke screen. I didn't inquire too closely, because I didn't want anyone to know I might have too much of an interest. Jake, I'm not an agent anymore, and I don't plan on talking to anyone else about this. You're my friend, and I figured I'd tell you what I know."

"Who was murdered?"

"A fairly high-level cocaine dealer was killed in Baltimore. The cops think Cecily was living with him. They also think that she might know who killed him, maybe even witnessed it. She disappeared before his body was found, and some inside the Bureau think she's dead as well. Their interest is in following the distribution chain and trying to nail the suppliers above him. His name was Edward Jimenez, known on the streets as Fast Eddie. He was selling quantities in the ten to twenty kilo range. Big bucks."

I looked at the CDs. "How did she get involved with someone like that?"

"A quick google of Cecille Buchanan turns up a wealth of information. Child prodigy, Carnegie Hall debut at twelve. Featured solo gigs with the New York Symphony at sixteen. Graduated high school at sixteen and enrolled at the Peabody Institute. She graduated college at twenty and had a solo world tour scheduled. And then, it was abruptly cancelled and she dropped out of sight. Almost nothing since then."

"I would have been in the service then," I said. "And when I got out, I wasn't paying much attention to the classical music scene. I had other concerns."

He handed me several sheets of paper. Leafing through them, I saw they were performance reviews from the New York Times, San Francisco Chronicle, and London Observer. The one from the Times was four years old.

Saturday evening, New York was treated to a performance at the Met by the foremost operatic voice to debut in this century. Cecille Buchanan defies the stereotypes. For those expecting a rotund diva, the diminutive teenager walking on stage was a surprise. But when she opened her mouth, she silenced the audience and firmly established herself as a force for decades to come. Her power is extraordinary, her range unprecedented. During the evening, she sang arias in the soprano, mezzo and contralto ranges without missing a note.

"When she dropped off the map two years ago, she had a contract with the foremost agent in the classical field. As far as I can determine, that contract is still valid." Dave said. "No wonder she gave me the cold shoulder. If she hit it big in popular music, we could have found ourselves on the wrong end of a multi-million dollar lawsuit."

"What you're showing me means money. I know opera singers aren't rock stars, but the top performers make millions," I said.

"Her parents control her wealth. Or at least they did until she turned twenty-one. As far as I can tell, she's very rich, and she hasn't touched it."

"Dave, what am I supposed to do with all this?" I felt lost.

"I can't tell you that. I do know that as long as the Bureau has a material witness warrant out for her, potentially you could be charged with either harboring a fugitive, or obstruction of justice. I think you need to figure out what she really knows, and then either contact the authorities, or find a way to smuggle her out of the country to a place without an extradition treaty."

He placed a hand on my arm. "Jake, even if she's innocent of everything except having bad taste in men, if the drug lords think she's a danger to them, I don't blame her for hiding."

When I left in the morning, she was singing along with *Salome* in Italian. Returning, I found a Grateful Dead album blasting through the house. I turned it down to a background music level, and almost immediately heard her bounding down the stairs.

With a leap, she flew into my arms, landing on my chest with her arms around my neck and her legs wrapping around my waist. I staggered, and the kiss she planted on my mouth almost made my legs give out.

"I love you, Mr. McGarrity," she said with a smile. "Guess what? I'm getting as fat as a pig. Will you still love me if I'm fat?"

I had to laugh. "I doubt that anyone would use the word fat to describe you."

"I weighed myself. A hundred five pounds. I've never weighed that much in my life." She pursed her mouth and looked down, then back at my face. "You would think that some of that would end up in my boobs. But I guess it's all landing on my ass. Will you still love me when my ass is so big it won't fit on a barstool?"

Since I was holding the anatomical part under discussion, I squeezed it. "I think you've got a long way to go before we have to worry about that. You're beautiful, Cecily, and I'm very happy that you're filling out. You were way too thin when we met."

"Yeah, not eating for a few weeks will do that for you," she said. "But still, I don't think it's normal to gain twenty pounds so quickly. Does good sex make you gain weight?"

I carried her to the couch and sat down, with her straddling my lap. "We need to talk, sweetheart."

She sobered. "Okay. You look so serious. What's going on?"

I reached into my coat pocket and pulled out the CDs. She stared at them as though I held a snake. Her hands pushed against my chest, and she tried to get up, but I held her firm against me.

"Cecily, I found out a lot of things about you today. I know about Edward Jimenez." She tried to get away again, her face twisting in pain. "No, wait. Listen to me. I love you. None of this changes that. Do you understand me? I'm not leaving you, and I'm not letting you leave me. If you're in trouble, we'll deal with it together."

She searched my face, and I guess she decided she liked what she saw there, because she kissed me. Slowly and tenderly.

"You're too nice for your own good," she said. "How did you survive in a war zone?"

"By being as tough as nails and faster than the guys who were trying to get me," I answered. "Cecily, we'll get through this, but it's time for you to be honest with me."

Nodding, she said, "Let go. I can't talk like this." When I gripped her tighter, she said, "I'm not going to run away, but I can't think when I'm this close to you."

I let her go, and she paced around the room, a look of intense concentration on her face. Stopping in front of the window, she asked, "How much do you know? What kind of trouble do you think I'm in?"

"I was told the federal authorities are looking for you. And that maybe some drug dealers are looking for you, too."

"Shit. I've checked, and I couldn't find that an arrest warrant had ever been issued. I hoped that maybe I'd gotten away with it."

"There isn't an arrest warrant. The FBI has a material witness warrant out for you. It was issued under a seal. In other words, it's secret. They seem to think that you know who killed this Jimenez guy, maybe even saw him killed."

She stood with her back to me, still staring out the window. "When I was in my last year at the Peabody Institute," she began, "I started having this suffocated feeling. I never had control over my own life. I started performing professionally at eight. A violin prodigy, they called me. I played Paganini at ten. There's something about my fingers and my ear that's different from most people. They measured me once. A neuroscientist at Johns Hopkins saw me play, and asked me if he could wire me to some machines. It seems my reaction time is about half of what's considered normal. I can move my fingers faster than other people. And I only have to hear a piece of music once to be able to play it."

She chuckled. "That really interfered with my development. It took me forever to learn to read sheet music. Anyway, when I went through puberty and my voice changed and settled, we discovered that I had an amazing range. My parents and my teachers were ecstatic. And I was excited at first. It's such a high to hit the notes of an aria exactly, and to be able to sing almost every female part is supposedly unprecedented. I spent almost every waking hour eating, drinking and breathing music."

She turned from the window and sat in the chair across from me with her hands clasped in front of her, staring at the carpet. "But that's not really healthy for a kid. I lived in an insular world almost completely populated by adults who pushed me to please them. And the more I worked, the more I accomplished, the more accolades I received, the more they always wanted from me."

For the first time, she looked at me. "I met this guy. I didn't know he was a drug dealer, but he paid attention to me, not to what I could do. He wasn't interested in music at all. His idea of music was rap. He told me I was beautiful and desirable. He took me home with him and fed me cocaine and a roofie and took my virginity. I thought I fell in love with him. I barely managed to finish my degree."

Looking me in the eyes, she said, "I didn't know what love was. Until I met you, I had no idea what it meant to be loved. All the drugs he fed me ... I get higher than that just seeing the expression on your face when you look at me."

Taking a deep breath, she gestured toward the CDs. "I had a tour booked after graduation. A thirty-stop, worldwide tour. New York, London, Paris, Rome, Vienna, Tokyo, Sydney. I would have made millions. Eddie said he didn't want me to go, and I cancelled it and moved in with him. He used to throw these big parties. Sugar bowls full of coke all over the place. He liked the way people looked at me when I performed for his friends. He was proud that he owned me, that he could show me off. That's the first time I played guitar in public."

She bit her lip. That was always a sign that she was making a tough choice and was afraid of what she was going to say next. "This is hard to say, Jake. You know, it isn't worth much to own something if you can't sell it. He used to trade me to men for a night, in exchange for drugs or other favors. Jake, I think you know I wasn't pure when you met me. I was pretty sure you'd forgive me for getting raped. I don't know how you feel about sleeping with a whore."

Forgive her for getting raped? "Cecily, I love you," I said. "You told me once that your past didn't matter, that I should just accept that you wanted to look forward and build a new life with me. If I dwelled on what you said, I could conjure all kinds of scenarios in my mind. I know what a woman might have to do to survive on the streets. I saw it in Afghanistan and Iraq. I don't blame any woman for doing what she has to do to survive. I don't care what you did before we met. None of that has anything to do with you and me."

She started crying then, silently, her lips trembling and tears flowing down her cheeks. She swiped at them with her sleeve, but they continued to flow.

"Eddie partied too much and used too much of his product. He got into a bind when he 'misplaced'," she made air quotes with her hands, "ten kilos of coke. It wasn't his fault, of course. Nothing ever was. I never found out what happened. I suspected that he might be gambling, on top of his other vices, but that's just me guessing. Anyway, his suppliers weren't very happy about him owing them a quarter of a million dollars."

Suddenly, she jumped up and went into the kitchen. I followed her. She took a bottle of whiskey from the cupboard and poured a shot glass full. Tossing it back, she closed her eyes and shuddered. Taking a deep breath, she did it again. I had never seen her drink anything other than wine, and never enough to get drunk. She gestured to me with the glass.

"Want one?" When I shook my head, she put the bottle away and washed the glass.

"The night he died, I threw what would fit in that backpack and ran for my life," she said, leaning back against the kitchen counter. "I hitchhiked to Nashville. I thought I might be able to find work as a studio musician. It took me two weeks to get there. I didn't have any money, and that's when I really discovered how cruel the world could be. But when I got there, I saw a report on TV that the FBI was looking for a mystery girl, as they termed it, who was living with Eddie. So I ran again."

"Is that where the nightmares come from?" I asked.

She gave me a startled look. "I didn't know I woke you up."

I nodded.

"I'm sorry, Jake." Cecily stared off into space for a few moments, then said, "I've had nightmares since I was a little kid. If I did something I wasn't supposed to, I had guilty nightmares about my mother finding out. And then when I lived with Eddie, there were people I knew who got killed. There's always an atmosphere of fear in the drug culture. A girl I knew was a dealer's girlfriend. She caught him with another girl at a party one night and made a scene. They found her floating in the harbor three days later."

Cecily took a deep breath. "I still dream about them fishing her out of the water, and sometimes the girl they fish out is me. Since Eddied died, I dream about that, and about the FBI and the drug dealers coming for me."

She looked at me straight in the face. "And I dream about some of the things that happened before I got to Greeley. I'm still surprised that I didn't die between Baltimore and here."

"That's why you carry the knife," I said. "I've never seen one quite like it."

"It's an athame, a witch's ritual knife. I guess originally they were used for sacrifices. Eddie gave it to me for my birthday. The hilt is a low-level silver alloy, but the blade is Toledo steel. He said he paid a lot for it."

The tears started again.

"God, Jake, I'm so sorry. I didn't know I'd fall in love with you, or that you would be so kind. I should have kept on going. You don't deserve any of this."

I took her in my arms and hugged her close. "I'm sorry for the pain you've had to endure," I said, "but I'll never be sorry that you walked in my door. We'll get through this, Cecily. Together."

~~~

Chapter 10
Cecily

Jake and I talked and determined that we didn't know what to do. We decided to call Thomas and ask his advice. But before making the call, I insisted that Jake take me upstairs and make love to me.

"Do you want it rough?" Jake asked as he laid me on the bed.

"No. I want you to be Jake. Remind me of why I fell in love with such a kind, gentle man." And so he did. Afterward, he called his friend.

There was a knock on the door and when Jake answered it, Dave Thomas came in and took the chair I had sat in while talking to Jake. I sat on the couch, my arms folded across my chest. Jake sat beside me, his arm around my shoulders.

"I'm sorry," Thomas said. "I assume you're not too happy with me poking into your business."

"I'm not going to shoot the messenger, Mr. Thomas," I said. "You didn't get me in this mess. I tried to find out if there was a warrant out for me. I can't say I'm pleased to find out there is, but it's a relief to know where I stand." I gave him a small smile. "Except that I'm still not sure where I stand. Jake trusts you, and since the feds aren't knocking on the door, I guess I trust you, too."

"I guess you want my advice," he said. Both Jake and I nodded. "Do you have access to any of your money?"

"Are my accounts being monitored?" I asked in return.

"Probably. You don't have any money that no one knows about?"

I chuckled. "I have about thirty-five hundred dollars under my mattress. I assume you're talking about more than that."

"Yes. I think you need legal counsel, the best there is. Did you kill him, Ms. Buchanan?"

"Mr. Thomas, I decline to answer on the grounds that it might incriminate me. I watch cop shows on TV. I know that you could be compelled to testify about anything I tell you. So, unless you're willing to sign on as one of my lawyers, let's leave what happened in Baltimore alone."

He nodded. "I know you're a musical prodigy. Do you mind telling me how you managed to enroll in Johns Hopkins' Peabody Institute at sixteen?" he asked.

I grinned at him. "And what does that have to do with the price of tea in China?"

"I get the impression that you're very intelligent. Whether or not that is true helps me determine how to explain things to you."

"My IQ was tested at 165 when I was fourteen," I replied. "I scored 1600 on my SAT. I graduated high school two years early. But intelligence is relative. Obviously, I'm capable of making some really stupid decisions."

"So are we all. As I said, Ms. Buchanan, I think that you need a good lawyer. To pay for that, you're going to need money."

"Correct me if I'm wrong," I said, "but since my money was all earned before I met Eddie, and can't possibly be connected to any criminal enterprise, the authorities can't freeze my accounts. Is that right?"

Thomas nodded.

"In that case, I can hire a lawyer. We just need to be prepared to move fast when I hand him the first payment. How much do you think this could cost?"

"Possibly up to a million. It depends on how complicated it gets, how long it takes, and whether they decide to charge you with anything."

I took a deep breath. "I can handle that." I heard a sharp intake of breath from Jake. "I'll tell you what I'm most worried about. Having some thugs with guns show up here. Even if I satisfy the authorities that I'm innocent of any crime, I have absolutely no intention of testifying against anyone. I am not going to help them put anyone in jail. I won't even give them information off the record."

I sat up straight and looked Thomas in the eyes. "I lived in that world for over a year. Eddie wasn't really a big fish, and even he had a fibbie on his payroll. I don't trust your old buddies. And the honest ones aren't above blackmailing a witness by leaking information to the bad guys. I knew a guy in Baltimore who walked out of a bust. The rumors started that he was a snitch, and he didn't live a week. If I need to move to Brazil, I'd rather do it now instead of going through all the bullshit and then still have to do it."

"I take it that you didn't partake in a lot of the product your boyfriend was moving," Thomas said with a raised eyebrow. "You don't seem to have a problem doing without it."

"I did some coke," I said. "I liked the first hit of the day. But it made me sick if I did too much, and it screws up my ability to finger the notes and it screws up my pitch. No matter what my morals are in other things, my relationship with music is as pure as freshly fallen snow. Even when Eddie threw his parties, he expected me to entertain his guests, so I had to stay sober."

Taking a deep breath, I said, "Do you have any recommendations?"

He handed me a piece of paper with three names and phone numbers. "The first name there, Donald Kerrigan, is someone I dealt with when I was with the Bureau. He kicked my butt on three cases that I thought I'd locked down cold. We had the goods, we had eyewitnesses willing to testify, and they never made it to court. I loathe the son of a bitch. But if I was in a pinch with nothing but dead ends, he's who I'd hire."

Nodding, I said, "Do you have some time? I'd like to talk to Jake privately. I can make you some coffee, or get you a beer or a glass of wine. Are you hungry?"

I made a pot of coffee and fixed him a sandwich, and then I took Jake's hand and led him upstairs. Closing the door to our bedroom, I said, "The same thing I said to Mr. Thomas goes for you. I can't talk to you about anything that happened in Baltimore. We're not married, and so our conversations aren't protected. Okay? It's not that I don't want to take you into my confidence, but I need to protect myself and protect you."

"We could get married," he said.

I took him by the shoulders and tiptoed up to kiss him. "No, that's a bad idea. That would make you and the bar open to anything that might land on me." I smiled. "Besides, that's the most unromantic proposal I've ever heard. You can do better. And I still might not say yes. Jake, I don't need a ring or a ceremony. If you think we should profess our commitment to each other in front of man and God, we can probably arrange to screw on a tabletop at the bar on a Friday night. A lot more people would attend, and it would be a lot cheaper."

He laughed. "Cecily, can you really afford a million dollars?"

"Jake, I had written off that money. I've been afraid to touch it, and truth to tell, you can't miss what you've never had. The last statement I saw showed about six million in my accounts. I don't know how much my parents might have drained from that, but they haven't been able to touch it since I turned twenty-one. If I get out of all this intact, without anyone hunting me, I can earn it again, if you want me to. And if you don't care, I'm happy with what I make at the Roadhouse.

I kissed him. I never got tired of doing that.

"So, what do you think I should do?" I asked him.

"Cecily, I can't tell you what to do."

"No, but we can make a decision together. Isn't that what people in relationships do? Are we in a relationship, Jake? Do you want to go through this? You can tell me to leave any time, and I'll kiss you and wish you well on my way out the door. You didn't sign up for my problems."

I think we kept Mr. Thomas waiting longer than I intended, but he was still there when we made it back downstairs.

"Can you make the call to Mr. Kerrigan for me?" I asked. "I assume that he would probably take your call directly, if only out of curiosity."

"Yes, he probably would."

"And I wanted to ask, if he were to hire you as a consultant on the case, would you be included in his umbrella of client-lawyer privilege?"

"Yes, I would. Why?"

"Because I need someone on my side. Someone I can talk to that the feds can't squeeze. Someone who will tell me if I hit the point where I need to cut and run. Jake can't do the first part, and Kerrigan can't do the second part. Mr. Thomas, I haven't done anything that deserves my spending time in jail or being killed. I'm not going to become a sacrificial lamb for the players in the drug wars."

"Yes, I can do that."

"Make the call, if you please," I said, and sat down on the couch.

Thomas left his name and number. We were kind of in waiting mode, since we didn't know when Kerrigan would call back, or even if he would. As Mr. Thomas was preparing to leave, his phone rang. He raised his eyebrows and nodded at us, letting us know it was Kerrigan. After a few minutes, he handed the phone to me.

"Miss Buchanan? I understand you have a problem," the deep baritone voice said.

"Yes, sir. It appears the FBI have a material witness warrant out for me in connection with the murder of a drug dealer in Baltimore. I have some concerns about my safety from said dealer's connections. And I don't know if the feds might arrest me and charge me with something if I arrange to meet them."

"I saw you perform at the Kennedy Center some years ago," he said. "I'm willing to provide a free consultation to understand the situation, if you're willing to sing an aria for me."

I laughed. "And here I was worried about how to pay you. Mr. Kerrigan, one of my problems is getting to you. I'm afraid that the second I present my passport to buy a ticket, I'll be arrested."

We worked through the logistics, and in the end, Jake bought a ticket to Denver for Kerrigan. We drove down on Sunday to meet him, and took him to dinner at a nice restaurant. But we didn't talk about the case.

After we drove Kerrigan to his hotel, Jake waited downstairs in the bar while I spoke with the lawyer in his room.

I told him my story, pretty much as I had told Jake. At the end, Kerrigan said, "You said, 'after Eddie's death', but you didn't say who killed him, how he died, if you were there, or if you did it."

Jake hadn't questioned me when I skated past that part. I took a deep breath and said, "He was stabbed to death. I saw him die. I don't know who did it, but I have my suspicions. And no, I didn't kill him."

He grilled me some more, then said, "I'll take your case. I assume you have the means to pay me?"

"Yes, sir. Do you want me to sing for you now?" I said with a grin.

He chuckled, but continued to wait for an answer.

"All of my money was put in trusts when I was a minor. I called the trustee earlier today, and verified that I'm now in control of them. He also told me that the feds got a court order and flagged my accounts. I can get to the money, but it will trigger a call to the FBI."

"Have the trustee transfer the funds directly to me," Kerrigan said, handing me a piece of paper. "They'll have a good time asking me where you are. Do you need any money from those accounts? If so, transfer that to me also, and I'll get it to you. We can use Dave Thomas as a go-between. Your idea of my hiring him was a good one. Now, here is how we're going to work this."

He went on to explain our game plan.

The dreams that night were bad. It was like a medley of Cecille Buchanan's greatest hits. Eddie, Alejandro, the man in West Virginia, the homeless shelter in Memphis, that filthy alley in Kansas City, and the trucker in Kansas. All the pain, the terror, the blood.

I hadn't dreamed about the trucker before, and I woke, writhing in the throes of an orgasm. If none of my other experiences taught me how sick I was, he brought it home in a way I couldn't ignore. How do you spend three days being terrorized and tortured, yet even the memory causes a massive climax?

Jake was holding me and murmuring soft reassurances. I wanted to ask him to do one of the things the man had done in my dream, but I was too ashamed. I couldn't go back to sleep the rest of the night because of the aching need inside me.

~~~

Chapter 11
Jake

I drove Cecily down to Denver and Kerrigan met us at the courthouse. At my insistence, and with Kerrigan's blessing, she was wearing a diamond engagement ring. She was linked with a dead drug dealer. I wanted to change that dynamic by linking her to a war hero, businessman and rancher, a pillar of his community in America's heartland. I also hoped being her fiancé would get me a little more consideration as far as access to her than being a boyfriend would.

She kept toying with the ring, looking at the diamond, then looking at me.

"Were you really a war hero?" she asked.

"They gave me a slew of medals. If they're finally worth something, then I'll milk it for all it's worth," I said.

"You didn't need to get such a large diamond," she said. Indeed, it looked a lot larger on her slender finger than I thought it would.

"I plan to recycle it sometime," I said. "In a more romantic setting."

That brought a small smile to her face.

"Jake, no matter what anyone says I did, or how disgusted you might feel, I really do love you. That part of what I've told you is real."

She didn't say anything else until she kissed me and said good-bye when we reached Denver. From the look on her face, and the fierce way she hugged me, I didn't think she expected to ever see me again.

We met Kerrigan, and then walked in to the FBI offices. Kerrigan introduced himself, and the agents who were there to meet us took him and Cecily inside. I had to wait. And wait. Kerrigan emerged alone three hours later.

"They've decided to put her in protective custody," Kerrigan said. "I thought they might pull something like that. Come on, I need to file a couple of motions with the court."

"What kind of motions?" I asked.

"First, an injunction to prevent them from moving her out of Denver. The second is to protest them holding her at all. The last thing we want is to have her transferred back to Baltimore. I don't think she's paranoid to have concerns about her safety."

"She was running scared when I first met her," I said. "She had all that money in the bank, and she had only eaten three times in five days. A lone girl hitchhiking across the country, staying in homeless shelters and hippie crash pads. She won't talk about it, but I've read about the drug culture. It seems they don't give a damn about human life."

"Baltimore is one of the murder capitals of the country," Kerrigan said, "and most of those are involved with drugs. I've done some research into her ex-boyfriend, and he was investigated in connection with at least a half-dozen murders. The cops never got enough evidence to arrest him for anything, but it gives you an idea of the environment she was in. When they found his body, there was a kilo and a half of cocaine in the apartment, along with marijuana, an ounce of pure heroin, pills, and enough guns to start a small war."

He went into the court clerk's office and filed his papers. When he came out, he said, "One of the things the agents pressed this morning was that she is a suspect in his murder. I think they're trying to pressure her into telling them more than what she's giving them. Your testimony about her physical state six weeks later may help. The cops found over a hundred thousand dollars in cash in the bedroom where he was killed. If she killed him, it would be inconceivable that she didn't take the money before she ran."

The judge handed down the injunction against moving her that afternoon. A date for a hearing on the feds holding her was set for two weeks later. For the time being, she was where she had worked so hard to escape.

The feds petitioned to close the hearing, so I didn't get to see her. Kerrigan said she looked pale and thinner than he remembered. He also described her as listless, until the judge asked her if she had anything to say. Kerrigan said she evidently had been rehearsing for that moment, and she gave the performance of her life. She told the judge that she had run from Baltimore because she was afraid for her life, named the FBI agent on Jimenez' payroll as justification, and castigated the feds for making her a scapegoat for their incompetence in controlling the drug trade in Baltimore.

"She also said that she had more faith in her war hero fiancé to protect her, than she did in a bunch of federal bureaucrats who couldn't find a marijuana joint in Baltimore with a flashlight and a roadmap," Kerrigan told me. "I liked that one."

So did I.

"The real zinger," Kerrigan said, "was her allegation of corruption within the FBI. The U.S. Attorney went nuts. The judge asked if she mentioned this in her interview with the FBI, and she said no. She said that she had been on the run from two criminal enterprises, the drug dealers and the FBI. She said she was afraid to talk to agents from the Baltimore office, or go back to Baltimore, because she knew there were more corrupt agents, but didn't know who they were."

"She's had a long time to think about all this," I said.

"Yes, and her reasoning is sound. There isn't a thing the U.S. Attorney can say to refute her logic. They have to haul the agent she named in for investigation, and they have to investigate her allegations that there are more agents on the take. If they send her back there now, and she gets killed, the stink will reach into the highest levels of the FBI."

He put a hand on my arm, "Mr. McGarrity, the judge asked her if she was well, and she said no. She said she can't eat because of the stress and her fear for her life. I moved to have a medical evaluation done, and the judge granted it."

"She was twenty pounds thinner when I first met her," I said.

"Christ," he said. "She's skinny already. She must have been nothing but skin and bones. Do you know if she has a history of an eating disorder?"

"Do you mean if she is anorexic? I doubt it. She's been trying to gain weight. She eats almost anything; she just doesn't eat a lot. She'll order a cheeseburger with bacon and give me half to save room for a slice of cheesecake. And she'll give me half of that, too. I mean, where would she put it? Even if she got fat, she still wouldn't weigh anything."

"Well, we'll see what the judge decides. They did allow me to give that violin to her. The FBI tried to object that the bow could be used as a weapon, and she asked if she was under arrest or in protective custody. She also asked the U.S. attorney why they expected her to tell them anything when they kept threatening to charge her with murder. Then she asked the judge if that was a violation of her Miranda rights. " Kerrigan grinned. "And then she said, 'Oh, I guess it couldn't be a Miranda violation, since they've never informed me that I have any rights.' The judge went ballistic."

I knew she didn't want her guitar exposed to the judicial system, but I figured my old violin wouldn't be a great loss. I drove back to Greeley, and sat around and worried.

Three days later, Kerrigan called me.

"Go pick up your girl," he said. "Dave Thomas will meet you at the jail and sign her out as my representative."

When she came out, she threw herself into my arms and kissed me. One of the guards handed her the violin.

"Good riddance," the guard said. "I hope you don't end up back here, missy."

Outside, I asked, "What was that about?"

Gaily smiling, she said, "There isn't an instrument better for conveying emotions than the violin. I've been playing funeral dirges almost non-stop for three days straight. One of the guards told me everyone in there is practically suicidal, including the guards. So when they came to let me out, I played an Irish jig for them."

What followed next were weeks of hauling her down to Denver to talk with federal prosecutors. Kerrigan flew out for every meeting, and I had images of the meter running and the charges piling up.

Now that she wasn't hiding anymore, she got a credit card, a cell phone, and opened a bank account in Greeley. I guess she transferred money into it from her trust, because she went shopping and bought herself a wardrobe that didn't include any cowboy shirts. The elegance of the way she dressed to meet with the feds made me feel rather scruffy.

One reason for the dress-up was that she took me to dinner in Denver or Boulder on every trip. The finest restaurants, places I didn't have much experience with. I could see the way she was raised, the kind of atmosphere she was used to. I protested that she was being too extravagant, and she said she was paying me back for all the food I fed her, and all the trouble she cost me.

Then she said, with a bright smile, "Would you rather punish me? We could do that instead." So I shut up and ate fancy steaks and crab and lobster.

But when we were back in Greeley, she put on her jeans and cowboy boots and acted like the girl I had fallen in love with. She wrote a couple of new songs about her time in jail, and sang them for the audience at the Roadhouse. One was heart wrenching, the other had everyone in stitches.

One day the phone rang at the house, and when she answered it, I immediately knew something was wrong. The conversation on her end consisted of a lot of 'yes, ma'am' and 'no, ma'am'. Until the end.

"No, I don't want you to come out here, and I'm not going to Connecticut. It's not that I don't love you, but obviously we don't agree on how I should live my life. And until you're ready to admit that I'm an adult, and we can have a conversation instead of a lecture, I don't think we have anything to talk about."

I raised an eyebrow when she turned to me after hanging up. She ran her hand across her face, and grabbed a hand full of hair and started pulling on it.

"My parents. Somehow they got your number," she said.

"I'm in the phone book."

"Well, that's kind of silly. You open yourself up to just anyone calling you."

I laughed. "So, I assume the conversation didn't go very well?"

"What conversation? My mother started lecturing me the moment I answered the phone, and I couldn't get a word in edgewise. In addition to being a drug-addict whore, I'm ungrateful, willful, incompetent to run my own affairs, and she demanded that I come home immediately so she can run my life again. Other than me being a drug-addict whore, there wasn't much to agree on."

I crooked a finger at her and she came over and sat in my lap. "I don't think describing you as a drug addict is accurate," I said.

She threw me a grin and said, "You're going to agree I'm a whore?"

"By some people's definition. You're living in sin with a man."

"Ooo, that sounds exciting," she said. "If this be sin, then give me my sin again."

CHAPTER 12
Cecily

I thought the low point of my week was the call from my mother. The visit from my agent, threatening to sue me and the Roadhouse for a hundred million dollars, trumped that.

I pointed out that there was a loophole in our agreement. I was allowed to perform at private functions for friends and relatives for free. Since my agreement with Jake was an under-the-table handshake agreement, and there weren't any records of his illegal cash payments that neither of us was declaring to the IRS, I told the agent to fly a kite. I dared him to prove that Jake and I weren't friends.

Jake looked worried for a while. I kissed him and told him to leave my money in the cookie jar from now on. "Honey, if they really try to make a stink of it, we can just tell them that I play for free, and you're paying me for sex."

The incident did spark an interesting dialogue concerning my contract and the possibility of my performing again. I pointed out that the contract was signed by my parents, and since I was over twenty-one, I wasn't bound by it anymore.

Actually, taking another look at the contract when I got home, I had additional questions. It was signed by my parents when I was sixteen. Although state laws varied, it might have become invalid when I turned eighteen. That brought up the question as to whether my parents were entitled to any of my income between the time I was eighteen and when I turned twenty-one.

I called Kerrigan and asked for a recommendation for a lawyer in contract law.

I was still meeting with the federal prosecutors in Denver once a week. Kerrigan always flew in. The FBI was excluded. The prosecutors' questions had long since abandoned Eddie's murder and focused more on what I knew and whom I knew concerning the Baltimore drug scene. I kept telling them that I didn't know squat on purpose. I never wanted to get involved in any of that. When people talked money, I always left the room.

Of course, all of that spurred the dreams and I was plagued with them nightly. Only now the FBI joined the gangbangers in chasing me. In the dream world, everything got turned upside down and intermingled. The night I dreamed about being gang raped by men in dark suits and trench coats was truly terrifying.

The bar was closed for Thanksgiving, and Jake showed me how to roast a turkey. Jared and Karen came over, along with two other members of the band and their girlfriend and wife. We still ate turkey sandwiches for a week afterward. I told Jake that I was going to fix Cornish game hens the next year.

The week before Christmas, the feds declared I was no longer 'a person of interest' and cut me loose. I steadfastly refused to testify in court and they got tired of badgering me. I paid Kerrigan off, and for the first time in nine months, I felt as though the air I breathed wasn't tainted by fear.

But it didn't make the dreams go away. As if my relief at knowing I wasn't going to jail released something in my guilty conscience, my sleep that night was bathed in blood. I might have fooled the feds, but I couldn't fool myself.

~~~

CHAPTER 13
Jake

With all of Cecily's legal issues resolved, life still didn't return to normal. The contract lawyer that Kerrigan recommended went to court and invalidated her contract with her previous agent. That didn't mean the guy wasn't interested in representing her anymore. It just meant a new contract needed to be negotiated.

Dave Thomas sent a CD of her original songs to a heavyweight agent in Los Angeles, and that agent also wanted to negotiate a contract. Cecily, being no fool, hired Dave to watch over the lawyer, who negotiated contracts with both agents.

I rapidly discovered that the little lost waif I fell in love with had a bit of shark in her when put back in her element.

"Jake, I remember everything I didn't like about every trip, every performance I ever did. All the fun things sort of merge together, you know? I couldn't tell you whether that sweet old man who was blowing me kisses one night was in New York, London, or Toronto. But I remember that jackass who said I couldn't play my violin in the mezzanine of the Toronto Hilton. He told me that little girls should be seen and not heard."

I loved the way she made me laugh. Life was never dull with her.

"So, what I'm trying to say," she continued, "is when we nail down the final contracts, I want to make sure all the constraints, the little irritants, are covered."

"My God," I said, "you really are a diva. Do you want a specific brand of lilac water supplied in your dressing room?"

"No, I want a certain naked Marine in my dressing room," she said with a grin. "Every night before I go on and waiting for me when I get off. If they have to pay him to show up, it's not my problem."

"Turning me into a sex slave, huh?" I teased.

"Darling, the slave role is mine, remember? Just be sure to show up in the right place, on time, whenever I want to be dominated." She winked at me.

I hadn't had a vacation since taking over the bar and the feds had taken care of my plan to take her to Hawaii for Christmas. A week before Christmas, Cecily breezed into the bar, laden down with shopping bags.

"Darling," she said as she stopped to kiss me before hauling her booty back to the office, "I had the most brilliant idea! What do you think about San Diego for Christmas?"

"I thought we were going to spend Christmas at home," I said.

"Oh, Jared will make do without us. If we aren't there, he can put a girl in every bedroom and play musical beds to his heart's content."

I heard Kathy and the kitchen crew erupt with laughter.

The San Diego idea rolled around my head that evening as I watched Cecily perform. I hadn't been there in eight years, and I was in uniform then. I knew the city pretty well, and decided we could have a good time. On our way home, I told her I liked the idea.

When I came downstairs the next morning, following my nose to the double bonanza of coffee and bacon, Cecily was sitting at the kitchen table, talking on the phone. I picked up pretty quickly that she was talking business, and San Diego was mentioned.

"Who was that?" I asked, munching on a rasher of bacon.

"The classical music guy. I'm setting up for all the agents and lawyers to meet us in San Diego two days after Christmas."

"And why are we going to do business on our vacation?" I asked.

She stood and kissed me. "So we can write the trip off as a business expense."

Pulling some strawberries out of the refrigerator, and bananas off the shelf, she began making pancake batter. God, I loved that woman.

We flew out of Denver with all the other holiday travelers two days before Christmas. It was starting to snow as we took off. Landing in San Diego, it was bright and sunny and sixty-five degrees. It wasn't Hawaii, but there were palm trees.

Cecily picked a tropically themed hotel on Shelter Island. It had the advantages of a great restaurant, a two-minute walk to the beach, and a king-sized bed. I took her down to the Gaslight district the first night and we listened to a jazz quartet in a small bar.

On Christmas day, we exchanged presents and spent the day in bed, letting room service feed us our holiday meal. I usually worked six or sometimes seven days a week, so having time to ourselves with nothing to do was a luxury.

She rented a conference room for the contract negotiations. They were contentious, with the two agents each wanting as much of her as they could get. She set a limit of twenty-five percent of her time as the maximum bookings that she would accept from each, including travel time and recording time. She also wanted assurances that they would coordinate schedules.

"No," she said when they objected. "It's not negotiable. I am not going to perform in Toronto one day and attempt to get on stage in LA the next. The resource you're arguing over is limited. For one thing, I need at least two days, preferably three, for my voice to rest after an operatic performance. I don't even talk the day afterward, let alone sing."

Every so often, she would turn to me and ask, "What do you think, Jake?"

I told her that it was her decision. After I gave her that answer a few times, she said, "Let's take a break, gentlemen." Then she pulled me out into the hall.

"Listen," she said, "I'm not asking your opinion just to hear myself talk. I'm genuinely interested in your input."

"But, it's your life, Cecily, your career. I can't tell you what to do."

"I'm not asking you to tell me what to do. I know what I think. I want to hear your opinion. Maybe you'll think of something I missed. Besides, it's not just my life. These decisions affect us, affect you. Or did I miss something? When I woke up this morning, I didn't think I was single. Has something changed?" She looked at the diamond she still wore, then looked back at me.

I smiled. "Okay, I get the message. You want my opinion, you'll get it."

"Great," she said, and kissed me.

It was finally decided she would do four two-month tours in the first year, two classical and two popular. Plus a three-week country western tour in the southern U.S. with Jared's band. She would also record an album with them and promoting it was to be a fifty-fifty job for the pop guy and Dave. I thought all of that was pretty ambitious, especially since no one had ever heard of her as a pop artist.

I underestimated the agents. When I flew back to Colorado, I went alone. Cecily was in the studio in Los

Angeles recording her first album of songs she had written. It made for a lonely New Year's Eve.

~~~

CHAPTER 14
Cecily

It was hard missing New Year's Eve with Jake. We were on the phone with each other, and being in different time zones, we celebrated the New Year twice.

The tour. Ten venues in two months, four on the East Coast, and six in Europe. A reintroduction of Cecille Buchanan. I would deliver an hour of Celtic harp, an hour of violin, and an hour of arias at each stop. The agent confirmed the bookings within a day of signing his contract. Smug bastard. I was hoping to talk Jake into going with me, but I also had a fall back plan.

I flew into Denver at the end of the first week in January. I had finished recording my first record of my own songs, and I was psyched. We also recorded two songs for internet release, a love song and a fun one with a beat you could dance to. There might be some background accompaniment added to some of the songs, but I would have the right to approve them before they were released. If everything stayed on track, the CD would be released the first of April.

I went down to baggage claim, and the handsomest man in the world was waiting for me. I flew into his arms and gave everyone a show. I had missed him so bad.

When we got in Jake's pickup, I slipped a CD with the finished songs in his player, and we listened to them on the way home. I had recorded violin for background to be added by the producer for six songs. But what I had was the final voice and guitar.

We didn't even stop at the bar, just drove past it and arrived home about six o'clock.

The next morning, I was fixing breakfast when he came down to the kitchen. "How did you like it?" I asked.

He gave me a lopsided grin. "I always like sex with you. Why?"

I threw a potholder at him. With my hand on my hip, I gave him an exasperated look. "The CD, Jake. Did you like the CD?"

He chuckled. "Oh, that. I liked it a lot. Did you bring it in with you?" When I pointed to my purse, he found the CD and plugged it into the stereo. It sounded a lot better than in the truck.

As I cracked eggs for the omelet, he came up behind me, put his hands on my breasts and pulled me back against him. I craned my neck to try and look up at him, then I turned, threw my arms around his neck and kissed him.

I shouldn't do things like that when I'm trying to cook. Men are so easily distracted. Pushing him away, I told him, "Go open up my carry on. I brought you a present."

"Computers?" he called from the living room. "Why did you get two?"

"They're his and hers," I answered. "The pink one's yours."

He came back into the kitchen and set them on the table. "Very funny. Seriously, why do you think I need a computer? I hate the damned things."

I took a deep breath. "I thought we could use them to talk to each other when I'm on the road."

"What's wrong with the phone?"

"With the computer, we can see each other. You know, it's like a video phone. And when I'm in Europe, we can still talk over the internet, and it's free. We can talk and see each other just like we were sitting in the living room together."

He considered that. "Do we have to be dressed?"

I grinned, stepped over to him and kissed him. "I can be as naked as you want me to be."

Returning my grin, he said, "You're making a good case. What else can we do with these things?"

"Surf the internet," I started.

"I don't own a surf board."

I slapped him on the arm and went back to the stove to check on our breakfast. Bringing our plates to the table, I pleaded, "Jake, come with me. Please? I missed you terribly when I was in LA. Why can't you come?"

He shook his head. "I can't leave the bar for months at a time, Cecily. Besides, I hate big cities. But these things," he motioned at the computers, "are a good idea. Being able to see you will be a lot better."

"Jake, you need to make arrangements to take off work next week," I said.

"And why am I doing that?"

"I need to go to Connecticut, and I want you to go with me."

"I thought you told your parents that you weren't going there," he said, a bit of a frown furrowing his brow.

"Yes, but I need to get my instruments. My violin, cello, and especially my harp. Finding another harp for performances would be difficult, and the differences between instruments for them are a lot greater than for a violin or a guitar. I also have an electric guitar, a Gibson hollow body like Jared's, and I like its sound better than his Fender."

He was silent while he chewed, then said, "How nasty is it going to be with your parents?"

"My dad probably won't be unpleasant. He may even be friendly. My mother will be a bitch. It's her normal mode, and if she decides to be pissy ..." I took a deep breath, "at her worst, I'm hoping that with you there she won't hit me."

His eyes narrowed to slits. "No one is ever going to hit you. Not in my presence. When are we leaving?"

"I made reservations for us on Sunday. My agent has arranged to ship the instruments back here, and we fly home on Wednesday. Is that okay? You won't miss any of the busy days at work."

"Yeah, that will work. She hits you?"

"Occasionally. When she gets really mad, she has slapped me. She scares me, Jake. I always feel like a little girl with her. I have a hard time standing up to her."

I could tell that he was deciding what to say, or maybe how to say it. Speaking very slowly, he asked, "If I was there, and you knew I had your back, do you think you could stand up to her? Make her see you as an adult?"

I thought about it. "Maybe. I don't know. I think I'll feel stronger with you there. But she's my mother, Jake. I've been thinking about this ever since I decided I need my instruments." Shit, longer than that. "Actually, I've been thinking about it since she called that day. I'm brave when she's on the other end of the line. I don't know how I'll act when she's standing in front of me."

"Cecily, I'll be with you every step of the way."

Chapter 15
Jake

We flew in to New York City and rented an SUV for the short drive to her parents' home in Connecticut. From what she told me, we would need the large vehicle to hold her harp and cello. Her family home was outside of Greenwich, not in the area full of mansions, but an upper-middle class neighborhood. Large McMansions on small lots too close together. Manicured lawns and expensive cars in the driveways. I may have grown up in cattle country, but my time at university and being stationed outside Washington, D.C., in the Marines had shown me how the other half lived. I didn't much care for it.

Cecily had called ahead, and her parents were expecting her. While we drove in from the airport, she was very quiet. That wasn't unusual for her, but in this case, she was tense and fidgeting. I didn't like her mother already, and I hadn't even met her.

We drove into her street and I stopped the car when I saw her address.

"Are you ready for this?" I asked.

"As ready as I'll ever be," she answered. "It has to be done."

"We could ask them to ship them to you," I suggested.

"No," she said, "I need to do this. I have to face them, and they need to see that I'm in charge of my own life. If I had the instruments shipped, they could continue to lie to themselves that I'm still a little girl."

I drove on and turned into the driveway. As we got out of the car, a man came out of the house and walked toward us. Mid-forties, about average height with light brown hair that was starting to recede, dressed in crisply-creased khakis and a polo shirt. When he drew close, he smiled and spread his arms.

"Daddy!" Cecily cried. She almost skipped into his arms and he hugged her to him. Then he grasped her by her arms and leaned back, looking her over and smiling at her. Her smile told me that her father wasn't a problem.

"You look great, Cecille," he said. "You've put on weight, and grown into a beautiful young lady. You look happy. Are you?"

"Yeah, I am," she replied.

He looked past her, and put out a hand. "I'm Franklin Buchanan."

"Jacob McGarrity," I said, shaking his hand.

Cecily cast a glance toward the house. I could see the apprehension in her eyes, and evidently her father could, too.

"Your mother isn't here. She said she needed to pick up some things at the store. She's been gone about a half an hour, so she should be back soon. Come on in. Your instruments are in your room. No one has touched them since you were here last."

We went inside, and Franklin offered us something to drink, but we declined. Cecily headed up the stairs, and I followed her.

As I walked into her room, I was tempted to shield my eyes. Stunned, I looked around in awe at pink and white lace. Everywhere. There were pictures of composers and musical instruments on the walls, interspersed with large photographs of Cecily performing in various concert halls. Fearful for my eyesight, I concentrated on those. I recognized pictures of the Metropolitan Opera in New York and Albert Hall in London.

She was very, very young in the pictures, and wearing pink dresses. In all the shopping that she'd done in

Colorado, I couldn't remember her buying anything pink. I wondered if the pink computer really was for me.

The only other things that didn't fit with the color scheme were instrument cases. Lots of instrument cases. A large harp case sat along one wall. Next to it was a cello case. I also counted two violins, a viola, a mandolin, a smaller harp case, and two guitars. There was a grand piano downstairs. Pianos technically are classified as a string instrument. I hoped we weren't planning to take it. As it was, I wondered if the SUV was large enough.

She immediately went to the large harp case and popped the latches. The case swung open and she anxiously inspected the instrument inside. Curious, I stood behind her and looked it over.

"How much does that thing weigh?" I asked.

"Only about thirty pounds," her father said from behind us. "The case, however, is another thirty. Cecille can't carry it alone."

In answer, she ran her fingers across the strings, and the sound filled the room. Opening the larger violin case, she looked inside and then closed it again.

"Can we load these in the car?" she asked, closing the harp case and gesturing to it.

"Sure," I said. I went over and picked it up by the two handles. It wasn't that bad.

I carried it down the stairs. Franklin got ahead of me at the bottom of the stairs and opened the door. He was carrying the two guitars. Cecily followed us with the mandolin and violin. I had a feeling that the instruments carried out first indicated their importance.

One more trip and they were all loaded. I wasn't sure what to do at that point, and Cecily seemed torn between going back in the house, or getting in the car. We ended up going back inside to wait for her mother. For two hours. It was a bit awkward, as Cecily wouldn't answer a lot of the questions her father asked. He looked embarrassed, and became more and more uncomfortable as time went on. It seemed that he glanced out the window every couple of minutes.

We could see the driveway through the picture window in the living room. Finally, a white BMW came down the street and pulled up in the driveway beside the SUV. A blonde woman wearing a white blouse and pink skirt got out, opened the back door of the car, and called, "I need some help here."

Franklin hustled out and she started handing him shopping bags. Bags from fancy department stores. From what I could tell, she was thin, like her daughter, with bleach-blonde hair. I thought she might be shorter than Cecily's five-foot-three, but it was hard to tell with the four-inch heels she was wearing.

We had called from the airport, and Cecily spoke briefly with her mother. It took us half an hour to get to their house, so her mother must have left immediately after the phone call. I thought Franklin meant she had gone to the grocery store or something like that. Obviously not.

Breezing through the house, she and Franklin carried the bags up the stairs. Cecily and I waited. Franklin came down about ten minutes later. Her mother took another twenty. By this time, I was past irritated. In my mind, it was established beyond all doubt that her mother was being deliberately rude.

Mrs. Buchanan strode into the living room, faced Cecily, and without preamble said in a harsh tone, "It's about time you deigned to grace us with your presence. Do you know how much worry and suffering you've caused me and your father? It's not enough that you ran off with that drug-dealing pimp, but when he got killed, we had FBI agents show up at our doorstep with a search warrant!"

I didn't like the woman before she got home. I liked her a lot less afterward.

"Where did you go?" she continued. "You just disappeared, and we didn't know whether you were alive or dead for months. And how did we find out you were still alive? More FBI agents. They come and tell us that you're singing in some dive bar in the middle of nowhere. I mean, really, Cecille. It was bad enough to let that pimp sell you on the streets, but to let this, this, cowboy," she gestured toward me, "degrade your art and pimp your talent is even more disgusting. I don't know how we'll ever recover your reputation. We'll be lucky to book you in dinner theaters."

"I'm not asking you to book me anywhere, Mother," Cecily said softly. "We just came to get my instruments."

"Oh? And are you going to play that harp in a bar? Are you going to sing Mozart to a bunch of ignorant cowboys with manure on their boots? Cecille, for God's sake. Wake up and realize that none of these men give a damn about you. You're ruining your life."

"I think we're done here," Cecily said, getting to her feet. "Jake, let's go."

I rose to my feet, looking around for Cecily's coat, and was slow to react to what came next.

"I'm not through speaking to you, Cecille," her mother said. "Sit down."

"I'm through speaking to you, Mother."

Mrs. Buchanan slapped her. I took a step forward, way past angry.

Cecily slapped her back, hard enough that her mother staggered backward. I thought she was going to go down, but her husband put out a hand to steady her. The shocked expression on her face was worth the price of admission.

"I'm through listening to you, too," Cecily said. "I'm through with taking your abuse, and if you ever touch me again, I'll knock you on your ass. I'll use my fist instead of an open hand. Now, you listen to me for a change."

She took a step forward and thrust her face within a few inches of her mother's. She was almost deadly calm and spoke in a fierce but measured cadence. "I don't care what you say to me, or what you think about me. But if you say one more word about Jake, I'll bust you in the mouth. And if I hear one word, one rumor, about me and Eddie, or me and Jake, or anything about my music, I'll have lawyers on you so fast it will make your head spin. I'll sue you for slander, and even if I don't win, the legal fees will drive you to ruin."

Cecily turned and headed toward the door. I was right behind her.

Halfway through the door, she turned, "No interviews. No talking to reporters. I'll sue your ass off. If you ever show up anywhere near me, or at my performances, I'll take out a restraining order. Do you understand me?"

Then she raised her eyes to her father. "Control your wife. I'm not threatening. I'm making promises. Keep that bitch away from me, and stuff a sock in her mouth."

We were in the car and I was starting to back out of the driveway when Franklin came out of the house and walked toward us.

"Wait," Cecily said. She rolled down her window, and her father went around to her side of the car.

"Cecille, I'm so sorry," he said.

"Daddy, you should have been sorry years ago," she said. "You've stood by my whole life and watched her abuse me. But I love you, Daddy. I've always dreamed of dancing with you at my wedding. I'll send you an invitation, as long as you don't bring her."

He leaned forward and kissed her on the forehead. "I would like that."

"How are your finances?" Cecily asked.

"Don't you worry about that," he said. "I just started back to work. We'll be all right."

"Daddy, send your bank information to the trustee. I'll transfer two million to your account. But that's the end. Understand?"

"You don't have to do that." The look in his eyes was a mixture of relief and humiliation.

"I know I don't. Consider it hush money. I'm serious. If I see one word she ever says to the press, I'll call in the lawyers. Put some of the money aside in case you ever get smart and decide to divorce her," Cecily said, then turned to me. "Let's go, Jake."

Franklin stepped away from the car and we drove away.

We drove in silence to the shipping company. When we arrived, she supervised the unloading of them from the SUV, and then stood over the men who packed them in bubble wrap and laid them in boxes reinforced with wooden frames. But the violin and the mandolin we took with us back to the hotel.

"They're small enough we can carry them on the plane," she explained.

"Is that the only reason?" I asked. She had both of them on the seat beside her, and she hadn't let anyone else touch them.

"They're the two hardest to replace. I can have another harp made. The man who made that one is still in business, and it's too large to carry. The guitars would be difficult and expensive to replace, but I can find replacements. The mandolin is a 1928 Gibson F5. The violin is a Mathias Albani, probably made between 1690 and 1700. They're insured, but where would I find replacements?"

"What kind of guitars were in those cases?" I asked, my curiosity shooting through the roof.

"A nylon-string classical, made in Spain in the early 20th century, and a Gibson hollow-body electric like Jared's, only older. I've played his, and they really don't sound any different."

"And the cello?"

She laughed. "It's ancient, Jake, an ultra-super-vintage 1979 model from an Italian company. The viola came from the same maker. The small harp was made by the same maker who made the large one. It's a commercial model, but the larger one was custom made. Don't worry, honey, we've got all the super expensive stuff with us."

CHAPTER 16

Cecily

After we left the shipping company, Jake asked me, "Are you all right?"

I had been very quiet. "Yeah. I'm sorry you had to witness that ugly scene with my mother. But I've had an epiphany of sorts. You know, ever since I met you, I've been trying to figure out why in the hell I let myself get entangled with Eddie Jimenez. I'm not stupid, Jake, but running off with Eddie was a monumentally stupid thing to do."

He glanced at me with a raised eyebrow. I almost giggled. He was such a nice man, and he would never say something like that, but I was sure he wondered what kind of idiocy had triggered the most disastrous decisions of my life.

"You told me that you felt suffocated," he said, his voice carefully neutral.

"Yes, but the fame, the pressure to perform, my agent, none of those were what was suffocating me. It was my mother. And I figured out this afternoon why I allowed Eddie to abuse me the way he did and why I stayed with him. It was because it was better than how my mother treated me. I was so used to doing whatever she told me to, that I let Eddie step into that role. When she said that you were pimping my talent, it suddenly made sense. Because you don't force me to do anything. It's almost like pulling teeth to get you to express an opinion when I ask you what I should do. The only thing you force me to do is think for myself, to make my own decisions."

I leaned over and put my hand on his arm. "God, I love you."

As we reached the hotel, I said, "I have a feeling that my mother was the initiator behind my agent threatening to sue us over my contract. That's how she thinks. One more manipulation to get me to do what she wanted."

When Jake and I got to our room, I took the violin out of its case and handed it to him. He acted as though I had handed him a snake, or a baby.

"Play it," I said, smiling at him.

"I don't play anymore," he said, trying to give it back to me.

"Jake, I'm not asking you for a concert. But you used to play. Aren't you curious about how it feels? It's only us here, go ahead."

He picked up the bow and tucked the violin under his chin. I watched him place his fingers on the strings, and understood how he'd been damaged. He told me he had some nerve damage, but as much as I had watched him, I hadn't seen him do anything that required such fine movement or touch. It was painful to see him try to bend his fingers and place them correctly.

Striking the first notes, he slid his fingers along the neck as he drew the bow over the strings. His eyes lit up, and I was so glad I insisted. Hearing a fine violin and feeling a fine violin are very different experiences. He played, his right hand doing fine, the left slow to reposition. After a couple of minutes, he stopped and handed it back to me, a smile on his face.

"Wow. So that's what it's like to play an instrument made by one of the masters. Play something for me, Cecily. Please?"

I took the violin. "I've been thinking of getting another violin," I said. "Later instruments are built different, and that started with Stradivari. His violins were larger and flatter. This one has been described as having a 'silvery tone', rather than the deeper and more powerful sound of a Stradivarius or a Guarnerius. That's the way modern violins are made, and modern violins have a longer neck, so you can play higher notes."

Tucking the violin under my chin, I gave him a grin. "But this one is perfect for playing Paganini." Niccolo Paganini, called the devil's violinist for his extraordinary talent, wrote compositions that were so technically difficult that others struggled to play them. I launched into *Caprice No. 24 in A minor*. I first performed it in Vienna when I was eighteen, and it truly launched my career into another level.

Jake sat down on the bed and listened. But halfway through it, my hand began to cramp and I stopped.

Shaking my hand and flexing it, I said, "I need practice. I'm going to have to be careful what I choose to play on this tour."

"I know my violin isn't that good, but you've been practicing," Jake said.

"Not three hours a day, which is what I did for years. My hand just isn't strong enough."

I had three weeks before my first concert. We agreed that I would do three-hour performances to display my talents. Forty-five minutes of solo harp, forty-five minutes of violin solos accompanied by the local orchestra, and forty-five minutes of singing arias. And as rusty as I was at playing the violin, I literally hadn't touched a harp in over two years.

When we returned to Colorado, I began practicing eight hours a day. The last night before I flew to Washington to start the tour, I waited until after Jake and I made love to spring my surprise on him. I figured he would be a little more receptive if he were relaxed.

Straddling him and lying on his chest, I said, "Jake, I need you to do me a huge favor."

"What is it?" he lazily asked.

I grabbed the tickets from the nightstand and presented them to him. "The favor is, don't argue with me, okay? Just be a good boy and say, 'Yes, Cecily, I'll come hear you play in Washington'."

"Huh?" He took the tickets, one for his flight, and the other for a front row seat at the Kennedy Center.

"You'll be flying in the morning of the concert, and flying out two days later. We'll have two nights together. Jake, I really, really, really want you to be there. It will mean the world to me. You're the reason I got this chance, and if you're not there, it will feel empty. I'll spend the whole time on stage wishing I were with you, and hating myself for being away from you. I'll probably screw up the whole thing, the critics will pan me, and I'll be washed up at twenty-two. A has-been. Please, Jake?"

He burst out laughing. "So if I don't go, I'll be the reason for all the failure and misery you experience for the rest of your life?"

"Yes. Poor little Cecily, her spirit broken. I'll probably start drinking and die of cirrhosis before I'm thirty. It will be a tragedy of cosmic proportions."

"You really don't play fair, you know that?" he said, chuckling.

"I'm a girl," I said, wiggling my butt around and squeezing him inside me. "We have to get by on our feminine wiles."

"Yeah, I noticed the girl part. Okay, Cecily, I'll go." He smiled. "Thank you. I do want to hear you."

I flew out the next morning. A week of rehearsals awaited me, and then my re-debut on Saturday night. And then I would go to sleep in Jake's arms again. That was the part I was looking forward to the most.

~~~

CHAPTER 17
Jake

I flew in to Baltimore-Washington International, arriving in the late morning. Cecily met me in the baggage area, carrying a dozen red roses and a heart-shaped box of chocolates, which she presented to me with a hug and a big kiss. I was profoundly grateful that Kathy had smacked me in the head the previous day.

"What are you giving Cecily for Valentine's Day?" Kathy asked as we were preparing to open for lunch.

"Huh?" I intelligently replied.

"Jake, tomorrow's Valentine's Day. Why do you think it was so important to her that you be together? It's your first one as a couple."

"Damn! I didn't even realize. Oh, God. Kathy, what should I get her?"

"Well, flowers probably won't travel so well. You know, if I were you, and of course, I'm not the one spending the money, but jewelry is always a hit with me."

"Such as? I tried to give her a diamond ring, and she gave it back." Cecily had taken off the ring and set it on my dresser before she left for Washington. She told me that since we really weren't engaged, she thought it was best to leave it with me.

"Jake, did you ever ask the girl to marry you?" Kathy asked.

"Well, no, not exactly."

She gave me a look with her lips pinched together as though she'd eaten something bitter.

"Not exactly. You're lucky she hasn't hit you up the side of the head with a two-by-four. And you weren't bright enough to take the hint when she took it off. God,

Jake, sometimes I wonder if you left all your sense in Afghanistan. Assuming you had any to start with."

"Okay. Other than a ring, what else?"

"Did she get any jewelry from her parents' house in Connecticut?

"I don't think so," I said. "She didn't take any clothes, nothing but her instruments."

"Well, don't you think a nice pair of diamond earrings and a matching pendant would look good when she's up there singing?"

"Yeah, they probably would."

So I drove down to Denver and went to a fancy jewelry store. Thinking about the computer, the tickets, the dinners, all the things she had bought me since she recovered her money, I decided that I really wanted to get something nice. Something nice ain't cheap. Something really nice damn sure ain't cheap.

I waited until we were in the limo—I had never ridden in a limo in my life—on our way into Washington, when I said, "Happy Valentine's Day, Cecily. I love you," and handed her the pink box from the jewelry store. She got misty eyed, and kissed me.

"Thank you, Jake," she said. "You are the sweetest man."

I sent a silent prayer to Saint Kathy.

She opened it, and her eyes got wide, her mouth opened in a silent 'O', and she just stared at it. Then she jumped into my lap and kissed me until I thought I would pass out.

"Do you like it?" I asked when I got my breath back.

"They're beautiful!" she said. "Oh, Jake, they'll go so well with my dress tonight. Oh, God, they're gorgeous. Here, help me put them on."

The dangling diamond earrings were pretty large next to her slender face, and the matching pendant hung from the bottom of her throat almost to her cleavage. I was glad I hadn't gone for a larger set I considered; it would have overwhelmed her features.

Looking at them in a mirror she pulled out from the back of the seat in front of her, she said, "Oh, Jake, they're so lovely." Then getting practical, "Are you sure you can afford this?"

"I only had to mortgage the ranch," I teased. "The bar is still debt free."

She shot me a look. "You're kidding, right?"

"Yes, sweetheart. I'm kidding. Look, Cecily, I'm not wealthy, but Jared and I aren't paupers. We own the ranch and the bar free and clear. When we sold the cattle and horses, we made a pretty penny. With the insurance money from Mom and Dad, I don't really have any money worries, and I've never touched any of it. The bar supports all of us."

"Jake, did I mention that I love you?"

"Not often enough," I said.

"Wait until we get to the hotel," she promised. "I'll make up for all the times I forgot to say it."

I had spent a lot of time in DC when I was stationed near there, but the Washington I knew and the one she knew were two different places. The Metro doesn't go to Georgetown, and even if it did, five-star hotels weren't something I'd ever frequented. Her room was large enough to shelter a small village. The bathroom alone was twice the size of my college dorm room.

We were barely in the door before she started taking my clothes off. Watching her as she rode me, still wearing her new jewelry, was a memory I knew I would carry with me forever.

We took a bath in a huge Jacuzzi tub, and then got dressed for dinner and the theater.

"I hope the tux fits okay," she said.

"What tux?"

"It's in the closet. I know what size you wear, but without being able to fit it ..." She went to sit in front of the vanity and began putting on her makeup. "Hurry up. If it needs some quick alteration, we can send it downstairs and get it done."

"You bought me a tux?" I had never worn a tux. Marine dress blues was the fanciest thing I'd ever put on.

"Of course not, silly," she said. "It's rented. But we'll have to buy you one. We'll get it tailored. If you can come to London, they have the best tailors there."

I wasn't going to touch that one with a ten-foot pole. I put on the tux, and it felt pretty good. I had no idea what to do with that ridiculous bow tie.

Sitting and watching her, I said, "Don't you have someone to do your makeup? I thought all big stars had people fawning all over them, doing their makeup and their hair, dressing them, wiping their asses."

She laughed. "Some of them do. They'll powder me and touch me up at the theater. But I've been doing my own makeup since I was six. I can do it faster, and I know my face. Even professionals tend to try and overdo me, and I'm so fair and slender that it looks like I'm wearing a fright mask."

I had never seen her wear more than minimal makeup, a bit of eyeliner and mascara, light powder and rouge. I watched as she spent over half an hour on her eyes alone.

"What about your hair?" I asked. "Are you going to wear it down?"

"Oh, no. I washed it this morning, and I'll put it up."

And she did. With a box of bobby pins and a couple of tortoise shell combs, she put her hair into a French twist with the same speed and skill as I saddled a horse. She then covered the twist with a loose-knit sparling net. When she stood and faced me, my little ragamuffin hippie girl was transformed into an incredibly elegant and beautiful lady.

Disappearing into the closet, she came out a few minutes later wearing a pleated gold and burnt orange dress, kind of Grecian looking, that hung from her shoulders straight to the floor. Her arms were bare, so that she wouldn't have to deal with sleeves when she played. The overall look was stunning. Slipping into a pair of four-inch stilettos, she said, "Will you please zip me up and hook my necklace?"

I leaped to assist her. She put her new earrings on, and said, "You look very handsome. Come sit down and let me tie your tie."

When she finished, she pulled me to my feet and turned me so that we could look at ourselves in the mirror. "I not only get to be the star of the evening," she said with a smile, "I also get to parade the most handsome man in the place on my arm. All the women will be so jealous."

Going back into the closet, she hauled out a long fur coat and handed it to me, then turned so that I could help her put it on.

"Where did you get this?" I asked. "Is it mink?"

"Yes, it's mink. My agent provides it. If you remember, I insisted that he bear all the costs of my performances. The dress, the coat, the limo and hotel room, all travel expenses. Even the makeup. That's why he's getting fifteen percent instead of ten. I don't want to mess with all that crap. My mother loved the frantic scurrying around, the shopping, all that stuff. I think it's a pain in the ass."

Turning to me, she put her arms around my neck and kissed me gently on the lips. "There's a girl, Myra, who's not much older than I am. She's at my beck and call, and she takes care of anything I need." She gave me a grin. "You'll like Myra. All the men do. But only look, don't touch, at least when I'm around."

"I won't have eyes for anyone but you," I said.

"If you don't notice Myra, and look more than once, I'll have serious doubts about you," she said, the grin growing larger. "If you look in the dictionary, her picture is right there next to the definition for eye candy. She's an ex-model, and she's really nice. Shall we go?"

We took the limo to the Kennedy Center, and went to the restaurant on the top floor. We were conducted to a table next to the window, with a view of the Potomac River. Georgetown, and beyond it Capitol Hill, could be seen in the distance.

I was a bit disappointed that we wouldn't be dining alone. Her agent, Marcus Neuberger, and the afore-mentioned Myra Cromwell were waiting for us. Cecily hadn't exaggerated. Myra was beautiful, tall and slender with large breasts and dark brown hair. Next to her, Cecily would fade into the background for most people.

As I held her chair for her to sit, Cecily murmured, "I told you so."

I whispered back in her ear, "Does she sing arias when she climaxes? I'm kind of hooked on that." Cecily giggled like a schoolgirl.

My seat in the theater was front-row center, with Myra sitting next to me. Every time I took a deep breath, I smelled her perfume. It wasn't unpleasant. To my great surprise, on the other side of her was Donald Kerrigan, who nodded to me.

Cecily's harp sat in the center of the stage, near the front, with a single straight-backed wooden chair and a low table with a glass of water next to it. A hand-held microphone also sat on the table.

The house lights dimmed, and a single spotlight found her at the left wing of the stage. She walked out, stood in front of the crowd and bowed. The applause seemed heavier than I would normally expect for an entrance. She picked up the microphone.

"Thank you for coming tonight," she said. "It's been a long time since I performed, almost three years. I've had some personal difficulties, but those are now past, and I'm sure they would bore you. I'm a little out of practice, so I hope that you'll be gracious and forgive any bobbles I may make. But I promise, I am going to give you my heart tonight. I never thought I would stand on this stage again, and seeing all of you here makes me feel more wonderful than you can imagine."

In the silence that followed, she took her seat. Lightly strumming her fingers over the strings, she picked up the microphone again.

"If you have taken a look at the program, and you're puzzled that you don't recognize any of the selections for harp, that's because I will be performing all of these numbers for the first time. I've never played my own compositions in public before. I do hope you enjoy them."

I looked at Myra. This was the first that I had heard of this. I didn't know Cecily composed classical music. Myra leaned close and whispered, "She insisted. She has total artistic control. It was part of her contract, you know. If she wants to play nursery rhymes or the Beatles, or change the entire program at the last minute, it's entirely up to her."

"Have you heard any of these pieces?" I asked.

Myra looked nervous. "No one has. Literally no one. She wouldn't allow anyone to hear her practice."

The first piece started with two strings being plucked, over and over like a heartbeat. And then a trickle of sound from the highest register, like a waterfall of silver bells that made me think of her laughter. The sound grew, and grew, until it filled the chamber, and as I sat and listened, I realized that she was telling a story. The music grew to a frantic climax, and then softened into a languid interlude before picking up again and sparking images of running through a meadow on a bright sunny day. When the harp fell silent, she mouthed, 'I love you.'

And then the hall erupted. Everyone was on their feet clapping, and calls of 'bravo, bravo' came from everywhere. Cecily rose, and bowed, and raising her voice, called, "Thank you! Thank you so much!"

When she sat back down and put her hands to the strings, the applause died down and she began her next number. She played four compositions. I was sure the third one told the story of Eddie's death and her flight across the country. It was dark, and dismal, with an early loud, heavy crescendo that morphed into a fast, frantic movement, leading in turn to another dark climax. It didn't repeat itself, but you could feel the progression. It was one of the most stirring and yet depressing things I'd ever heard.

The final number that followed evoked images of flying, a joyful paean to life and freedom. The contrast was so huge, that I felt as though I was floating out of my seat. The rest of the audience seemed to like it, too. The ovation when she finished, stepping away from the harp and bowing, was tremendous, going on and on for over five minutes. Other than stepping back on stage once to take another bow, she did not stay until the applause finished.

Myra clasped my arm. "I need something to drink," she said. I nodded and escorted her out to the lobby.

"My God," Myra exclaimed after we each got a glass of wine. "I knew she was talented, but that was one of the most powerful things I've ever heard. She plays the harp as though it was an extension of her soul."

"I don't know when she wrote those," I said. "Until three weeks ago, she hadn't touched a harp in almost three years."

The violin portion of the program consisted of her standing alone on the stage in a spotlight, with the orchestra in the pit. She played two concertos, a complex piece by Brahms first, and finished with a sensuous concerto by Max Bruch. I knew both pieces and her renditions were not only flawless, but passionate and inspiring. Again, the applause was thunderous.

For her vocal performance, she pulled out the stops. Not playing it safe, for her finale she sang *Casta Diva*, or *Pure Goddess* in English, from the opera *Norma* by Bellini. It was an aria closely associated with Maria Callas, and also sung by Beverly Sills and Joan Sutherland. For a young singer to invite comparisons to those immortals was a daring gambit. I was sure every person in the audience must have a recording of the aria by one of those three. I did.

It brought down the house. Cecily walked to the front of the stage, tears running down her face and ruining her makeup. She bowed and waved and threw kisses to the audience, over and over again. Flowers rained down on her. I felt a tug at my elbow. Looking down, I found that a smiling Myra was trying to hand me a huge bouquet of roses. I took it and walked toward the stage.

Cecily bent down and I handed the flowers to her, along with a handkerchief. "You're destroying your makeup," I shouted over the din.

"I don't care," she shouted back.

CHAPTER 18
Cecily

I was sure I had played and sang better, but I knew I had never put so much passion into a performance. When the last note of *Casta Diva* died out, the room was totally silent. I dropped my chin to my chest, completely spent. The silence seemed to stretch, and I wondered if I had chanced too much.

And then an avalanche of sound rose up out of the audience and rolled over me. I looked up, and everyone was on their feet, clapping and stamping their feet and cheering, calling 'bravo' and 'encore', calling my name. An encore was out of the question. I felt like a used dishrag.

Walking to the front of the stage, I bowed and raised my hands in the air and bowed again. The applause increased. I had never given a performance where the audience was so loud. I looked down at Jake. He was clapping and had a huge smile on his face. I could barely hear him as he shouted, "Fantastic! You nailed it!"

I looked back out at the audience and a flower hit me in the shoulder. People were coming down the aisles, throwing flowers on the stage, and then someone placed a bouquet on the stage. Something tickled my cheek and when I brushed at it with my wrist I saw a black stain. I realized that tears were running down my cheeks and my mascara was running.

Jake brought me a bouquet and I took it from him. He also handed me a handkerchief to wipe my eyes. I started to back up, in preparation for leaving the stage, but the ovation went on and on. The house lights came on, but the people continued to clap and cheer. Hardly anyone was reaching for their coat or looking like they wanted to leave.

Completely overcome, I fell to my knees and held my arms out to them. The clapping intensified again. Finally, Myra and Jake appeared beside me out of nowhere and helped me to my feet. They led me away, but just before I walked off stage, I turned and waived one last time.

Take that, Mommy dearest, I thought to myself.

Classical venues can't survive on ticket sales alone. The balance of the money they need to operate comes from donations from wealthy benefactors. For that performance, the tickets ranged from a hundred to three hundred dollars. But the theater had less than three thousand seats. One of the things big donations give you is an invitation to an after party, where the privileged audience members meet with the cast and the stars. It was a solo show, so I wasn't done yet.

Myra took me back to my dressing room and we fixed my makeup. Jake came in and hugged and kissed me, and then Myra helped me fix my makeup again.

Marcus handed me a glass of champagne when I arrived at the party. He looked really happy. I was hungry, so I hit the buffet and downed half a dozen toast points with caviar. I fed one to Jake, and he made an awful face.

"Don't you like it?" I asked, laughing at him.

"Not at all," he said, washing it down with champagne.

"That's great. I can keep it in the fridge and know you won't eat it," I said, eating another.

I shook hands and exchanged pleasantries with a couple of dozen people, most of them old enough to be my grandparents. Several commented on the harp music, and several asked if the music was intended to tell a story. I said yes, it was about my personal journey the past three years.

As the crowd thinned out, I was chatting with Jake, Myra and Marcus when Jake asked, "What was the story you were telling with that first piece? I think I understood the others."

I grinned and winked at him. "That was the first time we made love."

Myra blushed, Jake turned beet red, and Marcus guffawed. "Are you going to explain that in the cover notes when you record it?" Marcus asked.

It was my turn to blush a little.

When we got back to our room that night, Jake asked, "When did you compose the harp music you played tonight?"

"When I was in jail. Oops, I mean protective custody. The first three, anyway. The last one I played I wrote this week. I don't sleep very well when we're not together."

"You wrote it this week? How many times have you played it?" The look on Jake's face was priceless.

"All the way through? Twice. Once yesterday and once tonight. Why?"

He just shook his head.

I laughed. "Jake, how would anyone know if I made a mistake? No one ever heard it before."

We stayed in the room the next day until noon, eating a room service breakfast. I sent Jake down to the lobby, though, to get the morning papers. I didn't know if there would be a review since the concert ended so late, but I was hopeful. He came back with the local paper plus the one from Baltimore.

I picked up the Washington Post, and searched for the entertainment section. The review was on page three with the headline 'Buchanan Conquers Kennedy Center in Triumphant Return'. It was a glowing review, filled with praise such as 'a tour de force on the Celtic harp', 'a virtuoso performance on violin', and 'challenging Callas, Sills and Sutherland, Miss Buchanan claimed a place among that exalted pantheon with her rendition of *Casta Diva'*.

"My God, Jake. I have an admirer," I breathed.

Chuckling, he said, "He can look, but he can't touch."

Jake flew out the following day, and my little company moved up to New York, with a week until a performance at the Met. We had a Wednesday concert there, then a Saturday concert in Boston and one the following Friday in Toronto. Then it was on to Europe. I wouldn't see Jake again until my final performance in Vienna.

Marcus and Myra lived in New York. She took me out to dinner the first night, then asked if I would like to go dancing. I had been too young to go clubbing when I toured before. Indeed, I was too young to go out drinking when I was in college in Baltimore. The only bar I had ever hung out in was the Roadhouse. So I said sure.

Myra was a man magnet, so I got to dance as much as I wanted. I was exhausted when we got back to the hotel at two o'clock in the morning. The next morning, I ate breakfast, set up the computer, and practiced while I waited for Jake to call. I was two hours ahead of him, an issue that would only get worse when I went to Europe.

When he called, I took off my clothes, purposely positioned the camera to aim at my chest, and answered.

"Hi Jake. I'm a mess. I miss you already."

"Good morning to both of you," he said, laughing. "May I speak to Cecily?"

I angled the screen up. "I thought you wanted to talk to me nude. Aw, no fair. You've got your clothes on."

We chatted and he told me what was going on back in Colorado. I told him about going dancing the night before.

"Doing the whole nightclubbing celebrity thing, huh?" he said with a smile. "I'll have to look in the scandal rags in the grocery store to see what you're up to."

"I don't think any of the people in that club had a clue who I was. You saw the average age of the people at the concert in DC." I hadn't thought about how my going out might look to other people.

"Jake, you don't mind if I go out, do you? I mean, you know I'm not looking to pick someone up."

The way his face relaxed into the tender look that always made me melt gave me my answer.

"Of course not. Hell, I'm out at a bar every night. I'd feel guilty if I thought you weren't having a good time because you were worried about me."

The concert in New York felt better, to me at least. I was more comfortable, better rehearsed, and a lot more relaxed knowing that the harp section wasn't going to make people get up and leave in droves. Even on a Wednesday night, we sold out, and again the reviews were fantastic.

Boston and Toronto went smooth as glass and as we flew over the Atlantic, I looked forward to spending a week in each of my favorite cities. There had to be some way to get Jake out of Colorado so that we could spend some time in Europe together. He said he'd never been there, and I longed to walk in Paris with him, to show him the English countryside, take a gondola ride in Venice—a romantic gondola ride. The only time I was in Venice, I watched a couple riding in a gondola, wrapped around each other, occasionally kissing, sometimes pointing things out to each other. I had wanted that with an aching a fourteen year old barely understood.

~~~

Chapter 19
Jake

When I got back to Greeley, I had some sleepless nights. I missed Cecily more than I could have ever imagined. I would wake up and reach for her, and sometimes panic before I was fully awake.

The fear was always the same, that a faceless someone had taken her away from me.

As happy as she was to see me in Washington, and as happy as she was to be performing again, the next night she thrashed and whimpered. I had become used to her nightmares, but after sleeping alone for a couple of weeks, it was jarring to see one of them seize her in the middle of the night. I held her close, and eventually she quieted. I thought the dreams might go away once she was through with the Feds, but obviously that wasn't the case.

I never woke her when she was having her nightmares, but I wondered if that was the right thing to do. I wondered a lot of things. I did some web surfing with the new computer, and did a lot of reading about the drug gangs in Baltimore. I also read about rape survivors.

Jeri dropped into the bar one night when business was slow.

"I haven't seen this place so quiet in a while," she said. I noticed the same thing. When Cecily wasn't playing we saw a drop in traffic and revenue.

"My star attraction is entertaining elsewhere," I said.

She gave me an appraising look. "Star attraction in more ways than one."

"Yes, I miss her."

"Is she doing okay?" There was something in the way Jeri asked that made me pay attention.

"She's doing all right. Why do you ask?"

She shrugged. "I just wondered how she's doing back out in the big bad world without Jake McGarrity there to protect her."

"Why do you think she needs protecting?" I wasn't sure what Cecily might have told Jeri, and I didn't want to violate Cecily's privacy.

"Come on, Jake," Jeri said. "I may not be a psychologist like my sister, but I'm not stupid. She shows up here as a starving hitchhiker and then we discover that she's a famous opera singer. It doesn't take a genius to figure out that something seriously screwed up happened to her. She isn't an alcoholic or drug addict, so it had to be something else."

Jeri took a long pull from her beer. "I'm probably stepping way over the line, but I'm guessing she was running from an abusive boyfriend. I looked her up on the internet, and she had a promising career. Then she completely dropped out of sight for two years, and the next time anyone sees her is when she walks into the Roadhouse. To me, that sounds like boyfriend problems. The kind of guy who locks a girl up and controls her."

I looked at her, weighing what to say. Jeri's older sister Connie was a psychologist and ran the Rape Crisis Center at the university in Fort Collins.

"Jeri," I said, "her story isn't something I feel comfortable sharing with people, but I won't tell you that you're wrong."

She nodded. "Honey, I wouldn't hurt her, or you, for anything. And you know I'm not one to gossip. Hell, there's more damn gossip about me in this town than I can deal with sometimes. I hate it."

We sat for a couple of minutes in silence.

"Jake," she finally said, "I think you should encourage her to get some counseling. Don't push it, but support the idea. There's something eating at her inside. Sometimes I see her react to men like a rape victim would. That's an incredibly private and crushing thing for a woman. But like I said, she strikes me more as someone who has been dominated and abused over a long period of time."

I considered that. It fit in both with what I knew and what I had suspected before Cecily told me her story.

"Were you ever raped, Jeri?" I asked.

"Me?" she chuckled. "A guy I dated in college tried to rape me. Dumbass. I beat the shit out of him. I don't think he'd ever dated a cowgirl before. But I knew girls who were, and I listen to Connie vent sometimes after a few drinks."

"So you think that a rape victim and an abuse victim are different? In their psychology, I mean."

"Yeah, they are. In some ways the same," she said. "But a woman can be pretty stupid when a man convinces her that he loves her. And abuse doesn't have to be physical. In some ways, psychological abuse can be worse."

She bit her lip, then drained her beer. "May I have another one, please?"

I pulled her another beer and set it in front of her.

"Jake, other than Connie, I never told anyone about why I got divorced. I was losing myself. He hammered me verbally. All the time. Belittled me until I felt like I wasn't worth anything. Made me do things and act the way he wanted me to. Finally, I rebelled. Connie helped me to figure out that he didn't really love me, he loved controlling me."

What she told me made sense, and gave me a context to understand what Cecily had been through.

I made a resolution that when she came home, I would try to talk to her about getting some professional help.

Cecily called me after each of her concerts. Considering that I didn't get home from the Roadhouse until three in the morning, five o'clock East Coast time, that meant she was totally exhausted when I saw her in my computer screen. But she insisted that she wanted to see me, to share her triumphs with me.

And they were triumphs. I was able to read all the reviews on the computer, and the critics loved her. She was playing to packed houses and finishing to enthusiastic standing ovations. Marcus made plans to record the final concert of the tour in Vienna, and a CD would be released shortly afterward. Sales of her existing CDs, almost non-existent at the beginning of the tour, had skyrocketed.

She also called me on the telephone every day at ten in the morning Colorado time, but the late night times were what we both looked forward to. At the end of each late night call, she would open her bathrobe and say, "See what you're missing, Jake? I miss you terribly. I love you." And then she would sign off.

I was happy for her, glad that she was able to resume her career. In the back of my mind, I was also a little bit afraid. What if she became a big star again and didn't have room for me in her life? Maybe I should just sell the damn bar and follow her around. At least I'd get to hold her at night.

It was unbelievable how much I missed her. She was all I thought about all day and all night. I had my plane ticket to Vienna, and found myself counting the days.

~~~

CHAPTER 20
Cecily

London. I had always loved London. Being there as an adult was even better. I had performed my program enough that I was comfortable with only practicing the harp for an hour a day, and we had one rehearsal scheduled with the orchestra I would play with. Myra and I went out clubbing at night, and one day we went to Oxford and Windsor Castle.

The success of my concerts in the States had a downside, however. I now attracted press coverage and paparazzi with cameras.

We had barely checked into our hotel in London when there was a knock on my door. Myra answered it and I heard her talking to someone. Walking into the living room of my suite, I saw a man in a dark suit shove past her into the room.

"Miss Buchanan?" he asked. "I need to ask you a few questions." He looked back at Myra. "Alone."

I felt a numbness start to invade my mind, but fought to maintain some kind of clarity.

"Who are you?" I asked.

"I'm from the U.S. Embassy," he replied, which didn't answer my question.

"May I see some identification?"

He pulled out a little wallet and flashed something. All I saw were the letters FBI. I pulled my phone out of my pocket, hit Kerrigan's number on speed dial, and tossed the phone past the FBI agent to Myra. With a startled look on her face, she caught it.

"Tell the man who answers what's going on," I said. Looking back at the agent, I told him, "I think you're out of your jurisdiction. I'd like you to leave."

"I don't understand what you have to be afraid of, Miss Buchanan," he said, stepping closer to me. He towered over me, trying to intimidate me.

"And I don't understand why you're here," I answered. "I don't know why the FBI would want to interview me in London."

"It's a matter of national security," he said, stepping even closer. "You have information that you're withholding. Quit playing games, Miss Buchanan. Your attitude isn't winning you any friends."

"Here," Myra said, shoving my phone in front of his face. "Her lawyer wants to talk to you."

He looked at the phone as though it was a snake, shot me a nasty look, then whirled and walked out, slamming the door behind him. I rushed over and locked it.

"What in the world was that about?" Myra asked.

I put out my hand and she handed me my phone.

"Mr. Kerrigan?"

Nothing. The phone was dead. I looked at Myra. "He didn't answer," she said. "I left a message on his voice mail."

I smiled at her.

"Mind telling me what that was about?" she persisted.

"An old boyfriend," I said. "The FBI has been trying to get me to talk to them. I just thought it was over."

When I was in Washington, Kerrigan told me the FBI agent on Eddie's payroll had been arrested. Three more were under investigation. And to have an agent show up here, it was obvious what he wanted to know about.

Kerrigan called later and I told him of the afternoon's events. The dreams were bad that night, but different from what I had become used to. I was in Eddie's apartment, and he sent me back to the bedroom to 'entertain' a special guest. I was lying on the bed when my biggest nightmare walked in and dropped his pants. Behind him, a line of men stood, waiting their turns. They all had Alejandro's face. I woke up screaming.

The following day, Myra and I went shopping. On our way out of the hotel, we tried to detour around a group of photographers who were blocking our way. They were yelling questions at me and asking me to pose. I tried to follow Myra, but a man jumped in my way and pushed a camera in my face.

I stepped to the side to get around him. Suddenly, I flew forward and landed on my hands and knees on the sidewalk. Myra hurried to me and helped me to my feet.

Looking back, I saw my shoe lying on the sidewalk, the broken heel stuck in a metal grate.

"Wonderful," I said, looking at my skinned palms, torn skirt and bloody knee. "Now I need to buy new shoes, too."

I limped back into my hotel room, and we applied some first aid. My fingers weren't damaged, nor were my wrists. I had three days to heal, so I would still be able to play. I changed clothes and we snuck out the hotel's side door.

That night when we were leaving a club, we again ran into photographers, and I was almost blinded by their flashes.

Two days later, the story of my drunken stumble outside the club hit the scandal rags, with pictures of my fall.

"I hate those people," Myra said, while Marcus paced and threatened to sue everyone in England.

I thought it was pretty funny. Anyone with eyes and an ounce of sense could see that I was wearing different dresses in the pictures of me falling and the pictures of me coming out of the club. Yes, they doctored the club photos to make the dresses the same color, but they weren't anything the same.

The following evening, London time, I got a call from Jared. "Hey, how are you doing?"

"I'm doing okay. What's up? Are you Skyping this call?"

"Yes," he chuckled. "I'm a bit more computer literate than Jake. I saw some pictures of you today at the grocery store."

"You're kidding," I said.

"No, and I looked on line, too. You're quite the sensation this morning. Look, Cecily, I know I don't have any right to throw stones, but don't you think you should cool it a bit?"

I laughed. "Jared, take another look at those photos. I broke a heel outside our hotel and fell in the morning. The dress I was wearing that night at the club was completely different."

"Oh. Well, still, don't you think you should keep a lower profile?"

I tried to keep my voice calm, but I was angry. "When you stop drinking and picking up girls in bars, I'll think about lowering my profile. If Jake has any questions about my behavior, and whether it reflects badly on the Roadhouse, tell him to ask me when we talk."

"Jake doesn't know I called. I don't think he's heard about this yet."

"Well, if and when he does, remind him that if he was with me, he wouldn't have to wonder if I'm behaving myself."

I hung up. I couldn't remember being so angry. The stupidity of the tabloids and their readers didn't anger me, but for someone who knew me to pay attention to that crap was infuriating. I wanted to call Jake, but he would be at work.

When Jake called at our normal time, the first thing he said was, "Are you all right?"

"Yes, why shouldn't I be?"

"Everybody wants to keep showing me pictures of you falling down, so I was asking if you're okay. I'm concerned as to whether you were hurt."

"No, I'm fine," I said. "You know that drunks are so loose that they don't get hurt when they fall down." I couldn't believe he was asking me about that stupid story. Surely he didn't believe that garbage.

"Oh, okay," he said. "Next question. When is the alien baby due?"

"What?"

"Well, I thought I'd check off all the tabloid stories at the beginning so we could get along with our lives. Let's see, drunk and disorderly, pregnant by an alien, planning on defecting to Communist China, starting a cult that worships cowboy angels ... I think that's today's list. Would Miss Buchanan care to confirm or deny any of the above stories?"

I started laughing. "What in the world are you talking about?"

"I figured that if you were getting falling-down drunk, you might also be having an affair with an alien. Equal probability. So I thought we could get all of this week's stupid stories out of the way up front and we wouldn't have to talk about them anymore."

I was laughing like crazy now. I held up my hands. "I scraped my hands a bit, and the scab on my knee looks like I'm twelve years old again, but otherwise I'm fine. I can play, and that's the important part."

"What happened? Did you just slip or something?" The expression on his face showed he was genuinely concerned.

"I caught a heel and broke a shoe," I said.

"If you'd wear your cowboy boots, you wouldn't have that problem."

"Yeah, you're probably right. I don't think they'd have gone with that dress, though."

He shook his head. Grinning, he said, "Cowboy boots go with anything. Cocktail dresses, tuxedos, swimming suits, you name it. You need to start setting fashion instead of slavishly following it."

"I miss you so much," I said, opening my bathrobe. "If you were here, you would have caught me and I wouldn't have fallen. Don't you feel guilty?"

He took a long slow breath. "If I were there, you never would have gotten out of bed."

"See? It's all your fault," I said. "Pregnant by an alien?" I started laughing again.

The London concert went well, and Myra and I took the train through the Chunnel to Paris because I decided I wanted to experience it. Mother never would have done it. But considering all the hassle of airports, it didn't take any longer, and I thought it was more comfortable.

In Paris, I took a day at the Louvre and half a day at Musee d'Orsay. I also talked Myra into taking a boat tour on the Seine.

"I've never done this," she told me about halfway through the tour. "I always considered it a touristy thing."

"It is," I said, laughing. "We're tourists. But isn't it great?"

"Yes, it is. I rather like it. I take it you've done this before?"

"When I was fifteen. I talked my dad into it. Mother felt the same way you did. But I wanted to see if it was as neat as I remembered. I want to take Jake and show him all of this if I can ever talk him out of Colorado."

From Paris we went to Rome, and I talked the owner of a restaurant there into giving me the family recipes for ravioli and a mixed fish recipe. He asked me to sing an aria from Tosca for him in payment. Not a bad deal. I got the recipes and he didn't charge us for the wine. I couldn't wait to make them for Jake, and I hit the markets for the spices and herbs I would need.

What made me really happy was the CD that was waiting for me when we checked into the hotel in Madrid. Jake sent the album I had cut in California almost two months before. I put it in my computer as soon as I reached my room and listened to it three times. Myra hadn't heard it, and I watched her face as she listened to it.

"That's wonderful!" she said when it finished, jumping across the room and pulling me into a hug. "Can I come on that tour, too?"

"I don't know. Are you serious?" I asked. I had truly grown to like her, and having a friend along on tour was a treat I had never known before.

"Sure," she said. "I don't know how we would make it work. Do you have the same kind of clauses in your contract with your other agent?"

"Yeah, I do. I don't know what he has in mind, but he's going to need someone to do the kind of things you do for Marcus." I sent Tim, the pop agent, an email that night.

I was talking with Jake one morning when he told me that Kerrigan had called. Three more FBI agents in Baltimore had been indicted, and one of them turned state's evidence in exchange for a plea deal. Almost forty local cops had been arrested, and the drug networks in the area were falling apart.

I think Jake thought I would be happy. Instead, I was terrified. I emailed Kerrigan and asked what could be done to protect Jake. I knew he wouldn't take my warnings seriously, and I could easily see a bunch of thugs showing up at his door.

The dreams that night were really bad, maybe the worst ever. Men from Baltimore came and killed Jake, and then they raped me while I lay on his body. I woke up shaking and screaming at three o'clock in the morning and didn't even want to try to go back to sleep.

Vienna was the last stop on the tour, and the one I looked forward to the most. Partly, of course, because Jake would be joining me there. But the State Opera House was a wonderful place to play and sing, and it held such great memories for me.

We flew in from Madrid, and then waited three hours for Jake's plane to arrive. Marcus went ahead to the hotel, but I didn't want to miss a single minute of my sweetie. When he emerged past customs, I flew into his arms.

CHAPTER 21
Jake

I came out of customs in Vienna and heard a shriek, "Jake!"

A tiny package of energy ran across the terminal and threw herself into my arms, rocking me back on my heels. Cecily pulled my head down and kissed me as though she wanted to crawl inside me. I really didn't mind. It felt so good to hold her again.

She was wearing a sheer white sleeveless top with a dark blue bra, blue jeans and cowboy boots. Her hair was pulled back in a French braid, and she was so achingly beautiful that I couldn't catch my breath.

In the limo on the way to the hotel, she bubbled over telling me of the plans she'd made. I hadn't been around someone as excited since Mary was in high school.

"I have tickets to Strauss's *Electra* on Tuesday night," she said, "and tickets to *Anna Bolena* by Donizetti on Friday. I've never seen that one, have you?"

She didn't give me time to answer.

"I booked a boat tour on the Danube for Wednesday, and Thursday I want to go to the Belvedere Palace," she continued. "And there's a place that has the most incredible chocolate pastries. I hope it's still there. Of course it's still there. It's been there forever. And we'll just wander around and see the sights and have lunch in the little bistros and oh, God, it's so good to have you here!" She punctuated that statement with another long, deep kiss. I was a little embarrassed, glancing at Myra sitting across from us with an amused smile on her face.

"And the nights we don't have anything planned, we can go out clubbing with Myra. Okay?" she took up right where she left off before the kiss. "You know, when I was touring in Europe before, I was just a kid. It's ever so much more fun to be an adult. I like going to the clubs and dancing. There's so much energy in the air! Do you know how to dance? I mean not-country dancing. Oh, it doesn't matter. It's not hard. You just shake your ass and get into the beat."

I pulled her to me and silenced her with another kiss, filling my nose with her scent.

At the hotel, Cecily turned to Myra and said, "Will you please find out where we can rent a tuxedo?"

"We don't need to do that," I said.

Her brow furrowed. "Jake, there's a dress code for the opera and my performance."

"I bought one."

"You bought a tuxedo?" She looked surprised.

"Yes, I went down to Denver and bought one and had it tailored. I figured I was probably going to be wearing one a lot, and it seems silly to keep renting one."

"I love you," she said. "Myra, what time are we going to dinner?"

"Eight o'clock. You need to meet us in the lobby around seven-thirty."

"Okay," Cecily said, and kicked the door to our room closed. Turning to me, she began unbuttoning my shirt. "You know what I missed most the past two months?"

One thing about Cecily, she was punctual. We arrived in the lobby at seven-thirty on the dot, although her hair was still a little damp from the shower. I assumed we were going somewhere fancy, as she told me to wear my best suit and she wore an incredible teal evening gown with the diamonds I gave her. Although Cecily didn't need a bra, her breasts were fairly large in relation to how slender she was. The dress certainly showed off what she had.

The limo took us to the city park and an elegant old building overlooking a canal. The inside was even more fabulous than the outside.

On the way, I said, "Something you didn't tell me is why my ticket was only one way."

"That's because we're going to spend Sunday after my performance in bed, that's my quiet day, you know. Marcus and Myra are flying back to New York on Monday. Then we'll kick around Vienna for a couple of days and fly to Paris for a week."

"Why Paris?"

"Because it's the most romantic city in the world," she said, with an exasperated expression.

"And?"

Myra mumbled, "Quit while you're ahead."

I looked at Marcus, who was giving me a look that plainly said, 'how stupid are you?'

"Oh," I said. "That sounds like a wonderful idea."

Cecily shook her head. "Don't do that, Jake. People will think you're slow." She winked at me and gave us all one of her imp grins. "And we know you're only slow when I ask you to be."

I felt my face turn scorching hot, and saw that Marcus and Myra also blushed.

When we sat down in the restaurant, Cecily pointed to my menu and started to explain the dishes to me. Then she stopped. "Oh, your menu is in English."

Looking around, I saw that everyone's menu was in English except hers. She had spoken to the maître d'hôtel in German when we arrived and while he was seating us.

"I didn't know you spoke German," I said.

"German, French, Spanish, Italian, hell, everywhere we've been she speaks the language," Myra said. "We went to hole-in-the-wall cafes in Paris and Rome and had the most incredible meals. Places where they never see Americans. You should see her in the markets. My God, she's a shark. She barters like a grandmother."

"You should see her negotiate a contract," Marcus said.

"You don't expect me to sing a song I don't understand, do you?" Cecily asked. "I know that opera singers do it all the time, but often their accents are so off that it's laughable. I'd be embarrassed to sing an Italian opera in Italy if the audience was laughing at me."

She took a sip of her wine. "Of course, when you're homeschooled, you just have to meet the state's minimum standards. Beyond that, you can study anything you want. Having an urbane multi-lingual daughter was something my mother valued. And I've been traveling to these countries all my life."

Over dinner, I asked, "What's so special about Vienna? You've been excited about this performance ever since the tour was announced."

"Wait until you see the opera house," Cecily said. "It's incredible. The acoustics are absolutely top notch. But it's also the only place I've ever sung a whole opera. Over Christmas break when I was eighteen, I was cast as Susanna in *The Marriage of Figaro* at the State Opera House. I sang six performances." Her face took on a far-away beatific expression. "It was wonderful. It was probably the best time in my whole life until I met you."

While I never got tired of hearing that sort of thing from her, it always embarrassed me a little. Even more so when Myra said, "You have a brother, don't you? Is he as wonderful as you are?"

I chuckled, but Cecily barked out a laugh, choked, and coughed into her napkin.

When she finally got her breath, she said with an evil grin, "Oh, Myra, Jared is far more handsome. Would you like to join his harem? It seems he always has room for one more."

Later, when we got back to our room, I teased her. "So, you think Jared is more handsome than I am?"

She removed her dress and tossed it on the bed. Walking over to me, she put her arms around my waist, kissed me on the chest, and then pressed her body against me.

"You're handsome enough that you can have any woman you want," she said. "It's like if you said that Myra is prettier than I am. It's true, but it doesn't mean I'm not pretty. You're a lot more than your looks, but sometimes I'm not sure if Jared is."

I kissed her, and then said with a grin, "Well, I'm glad you don't see me as just another pretty face."

"Oh, your face is very pretty. I never get tired of looking at you. It's sort of a bonus, because that's not why I love you."

She and Myra took me out 'clubbing', as they called it, a couple of nights. When I was in college, we called it bar hopping. I did think it was kind of funny that Cecily thought I had never been in a bar that didn't play cowboy music. I had to admit, it was a huge boost to my ego to walk into a bar with those two on my arms.

The second evening we went dancing, we were met by camera flashes as we came out of a club. There had been photographers outside our hotel earlier that day, and also outside the opera house when Cecily showed up for rehearsal.

"Damn, I hate those vultures!" Myra said.

"If you can't stand the heat, don't hang around with celebrities," Cecily said through gritted teeth. Then she struck a pose for them, opening her coat so they could see her dress, turning slightly to the side so her breasts showed better, and flashing them a smile.

"Thank you so much for coming," she called.

Myra and I grabbed her and pulled her into the limo. She laughed like a crazy woman, saying, "I wonder what kind of bullshit they'll print tomorrow."

The following morning, we were still in bed when Cecily got a text from Myra with an internet link. Opening her laptop, Cecily typed in the URL and stared at the screen for a minute. She burst out laughing.

"What is it?" I asked.

She was laughing so hard she couldn't answer, so she pushed the screen around so I could read it. I noted it was the website of the tabloid that printed the falling-down-drunk story.

'Cecille Buchanan, the darling diva and new superstar of the classical music set, is continuing to party her way across Europe. In Vienna this week, her constant companion is a mystery European hunk who, according to hotel staff, is sharing her hotel room. Seen here, they danced until dawn at Vienna's hottest nightclub before her limo whisked them away. There has been no official word from the 23 year old Miss Buchanan's camp about the state of her engagement to Colorado rancher Jake McGarrity, but knowledgeable sources note that she has not been wearing her engagement ring.'

The pictures with the story included several of her and me together, including going into and coming out of the club, and a close up of her left hand as she got in the limo.

"You haven't been wearing a ring since you left Colorado," I said. It also irked me that we left the club just after midnight, not dawn.

"Oh, my God, I've been busted!" she gasped between bouts of laughter. "How am I ever going to explain this to Jake?"

The story sparked one thing for me, however. "Cecily, you're twenty-three?"

"Yes," she said, still smiling but with a questioning look on her face.

"When is your birthday?"

She instantly sobered. "Oh, I guess I never did tell you that. July tenth."

I tried to think back to what we were doing that day. "Was that the day ..."

She leaned forward and kissed me. "Yes, that's the day I said I was moving out. The day we told each other that we loved each other and made love the first time. It was the best birthday of my life."

Marcus arranged for Cecily's performance to be recorded and videotaped. They would be selling both the recording as well as the video, and he was in negotiations to have the video run on public broadcasting TV stations.

For the performance, she wore a red evening gown almost exactly like the teal one she wore to dinner my first night in Vienna. Myra and a hairdresser did her hair in what they called an inverse French braid, which was very elegant. She looked spectacular, and in the State Opera House, with its five tiers of balconies surrounding the theater, everyone had a good seat. Seven cameras were set up, and I could imagine what the editing would be like.

As in Washington, Myra and I sat front row center, but that was still fairly far from the stage since the orchestra pit was very wide and shallow. I was glad that I had several chances that week to roam around while Cecily was rehearsing, because the hall itself was spectacular. There literally wasn't a bad seat in the house, even from the top tier of the fifth balcony. I was sure it would make a fantastic video.

While her performance in Washington had more passion, from a technical standpoint the performance in Vienna was flawless. And when shouts of 'encore' at the end rang through the chamber, she came back on stage with her harp.

I didn't understand what she said, because I don't speak German, but whatever it was, the crowd resumed their seats expectantly.

"Oh, my God," Myra whispered to me. "She's going to do something she just wrote this week, something she's never performed before."

"When did she have time to write something?" I whispered back. "I've been with her every minute."

The prelude on the harp was beautiful, cascading waterfalls of sound, and then she began to sing. It was a love song, in English, sung in high operatic style. Stunned, I listened to the lyrics,
hearing my name ring through the chamber as the final line, "Jacob, I love you," died out. It was a groundbreaking performance. In the classical world, no one gets on stage solo and sings while they play, let alone play their own compositions.

I wasn't ashamed at the tears that I felt running down my cheeks.

~~~

CHAPTER 22
Cecily

A week in Paris with Jake was everything I dreamed it would be. Without any publicity about my itinerary, and staying at a small boutique hotel, we completely avoided the press. We walked around town, did all the touristy things, saw the museums, and saw a performance at the opera house. For the first time, I had him all to myself with no schedules, no work, no responsibilities and no one else that we needed to please.

On the plane, he admitted that he enjoyed the vacation, and would like to see more of Europe.

"Then you'll come with me for the fall tour?" I asked hopefully.

"No, honey. I can't be gone that long. But I'll come and hear you a couple of times, and we can plan another vacation if you wish."

"Jake, couldn't you hire a manager for the bar?"

"Of course I could, but I don't want to. Cecily, touring and performing is your dream, not mine. I could have sold the bar if I wanted to do something else or go somewhere else. I'm happy there. I'll keep our home warm and waiting for you."

"Our home, Jake?"

"I hope so. I hope you'll stay with me now that you're rich and famous."

I thought about that for a while. It didn't matter to me where I lived, as long as it was with him. After this year, I was committed to spending half my time performing and recording. That meant half my time away from him.

"If it's our home," I ventured, "can I build something there?"

He cocked his head and looked at me with a look of amusement on his face. "What do you want to build?"

"A recording studio. I could do most of my recording there, and Jared could use it, too. If I need an orchestra, I can go to Denver. But that would keep me home more. As it is now, I recorded that album in California, we're going to record my country album and the band's album in Nashville, and Marcus wants me to record a classical album in New York. I could be spending all that time in my own bed."

He smiled. "I think that's a wonderful idea. Can you afford it?"

"I've been checking," I said. "It's really not that expensive. We can build and equip a really good one for a couple of hundred thousand."

"Well, let's get started on it when we get back," he said.

He called an architect friend of his when we got back to Greeley, and the guy came out and talked to me. Then he went away to do some research and work on plans. Something I hadn't known was that Jared had a degree in structural engineering. When I told him what I planned, he jumped in and took over the project. Together, we researched equipment and acoustics.

It was sort of a revelation. In spite of being around him a lot, I really didn't know him very well. I had always seen him as a womanizing party boy, but he was smart and had a serious side.

I barely had time to unpack before I was off again to Nashville to record my country album with Jared's band. And the band also recorded their own album. We wrapped both of them in three weeks, then I had two weeks at home before I started my solo tour promoting my pop album. Twenty cities in sixty days. At most of the stops, I opened for more well-known acts.

Myra called on my second day back in Greeley.

"Cecily, your lawyer should be sending you amended contracts to sign," she said. "Tim and Marcus are kicking back part of their cuts, and if you agree, I'll be working for you from now on."

"Oh? Are you okay with that?" I asked.

"I worked for you this winter. I mean you weren't paying me directly, but about ninety percent of what I did was directly for you. Are you okay with it?"

"So I'll be responsible for your travel and living expenses? And how are you going to get paid when I'm not touring?" I asked. "You were a full-time employee of Marcus's company, weren't you?"

"I can keep your schedule, answer your fan mail, play secretary, maintain your website, coordinate your travel, you know, whatever you need done." I could hear a hopeful, pleading note in her voice.

"How much am I paying you?"

She hesitated. "Marcus was paying me sixty thousand," she finally said. "I was hoping I could talk you into a hundred."

"Are you willing to move to Colorado?" I asked.

"Yes, of course."

"Have you ever been to Greeley, Colorado?" I couldn't imagine a place more different from New York.

"No," she said in a small voice. "It's near Denver, isn't it?"

"About an hour away. Come on out, and we'll talk about it," I said.

Jake and I discussed it that night.

"She could probably live in Denver," Jake said after I explained everything. "It's not New York, either, but for a city girl, it's a lot closer to what she's used to than Greeley. Does she know how to drive?"

"I think so," I said. "She grew up in a suburb of Pittsburg, so she probably does."

Myra flew in on Saturday, rented a car, and drove to Greeley. We put her in Mary's room, and I took her to the Roadhouse that night. It hadn't really occurred to me before how much Myra and Jeri looked alike. They were of similar height, their hair was the same color, and if Jeri was five years younger and twenty pounds lighter, they could have been twins. Watching them together that night, I understood why Jake always seemed so uncomfortable around Myra. He must have been seeing Jeri when he was in love with her.

Tim, the pop agent, put together a backup band for me. Electric bass, rhythm guitar, electric piano, and a violin. I didn't meet the musicians or get to play with them until the week before the Denver concert. I picked them from recordings he sent me and interviews I conducted over the phone. They flew into Denver and came to Greeley on Sunday, and we practiced at the Roadhouse during the day and played in the evenings.

By Friday night, we sounded pretty good together. It was our only end-to-end dress rehearsal, and we played two hour-long sets. I did about half a dozen songs completely solo, and I could do them all that way if I needed to.

After we finished playing, I ate dinner with Jake, then got back on the stage and took requests, the way I used to do every evening. I knew most of the people in the audience, and it felt like coming home.

When I finished with my final set, I walked over to the table where Jeri, Myra and Terrie, the violin player with my band, were sitting. It was kind of an odd feeling. I had never had girlfriends. I considered at least two of these women as friends. I wasn't sure about Terrie yet.

"I never get tired of listening to you sing," Jeri said, drawing me into a quick hug. "Damn, girl, you sound like you swallowed an angel."

I laughed. "I'm no angel. He's over there behind the bar."

They all turned and looked at Jake.

"Listening to her, you'd think he walked on water," Myra said with a laugh.

Jeri shot a glance at me, and then looked at Myra. "Everyone has their own savior," she said, then looked back at me and captured my eyes. "There's love, and sometimes there are things beyond love."

I licked my lips, not really sure what to say. He was everything to me, and I brought him nothing but trouble. I couldn't even stay home with him like I should.

Suddenly I realized that the table had gone quiet and somber. "I'll buy the next round," I said, jumping up and walking over to the bar to tell Jake.

I started the tour in Denver so Jake could come. So did Kathy, Jeri, Jared and all the band members, and a bunch of my friends from Greeley. Jake posted promos for the concert all over town and he closed the bar that night.

We opened for a group that primarily consisted of two lesbian women, though they had a backup band. They had several top hits and several albums and had been recording and touring for at least ten or fifteen years. Tim hoped my music would resonate with their fans.

Most of the people attending had probably never heard of me. I started out with one of the songs the band played with me, the song that had the most internet hits. It started with a spotlight on Darlene playing the piano introduction. Then when the rest of the band cut in and I started to sing, the lights on the stage came on and three spots focused on me. I knew what they saw. A little blonde girl with a large guitar, standing there and hoping to make good.

It was by far the largest venue I had ever played, but I had confidence in my voice. With a microphone, I figured I could blow the roof off. The crowd was restless and excited, anticipating good music and a good time. I thought of Jake telling me that as long as I didn't sound like a tortured cat, he would let me sing for my dinner.

I opened my mouth, and did my best to let everyone know I belonged there. I sang one more number backed up by the band, and then the lights focused only on me. Playing the Martin, I sang the song I had written for Jake, the song I played on harp for my encore in Vienna. The song was modified to a narrower vocal range, the tune re-written for guitar and a folk-pop audience. I had never heard such applause and cheering in my life. These people were a lot less restrained than classical or operatic audiences. Smiling my fool head off, I decided I could get used to it.

Ed, my guitar player, stepped up and shouted in my ear, "Screw what we planned. Do a malaguena, then do *Wandering Traveler*, and then we'll step back in and hit them with *Dance All Night*."

I looked at him, then at the audience. "Are you sure?"

"Trust me," he said. He had done gigs with some of the biggest names in the business. I pulled a stool over, and changed to my classical guitar. A malaguena is a type of flamenco music from southern Spain. As I hit the first few notes, the audience quieted. I played through it, giving an American audience a taste of how powerful an acoustic guitar could be. While the notes were still dying away, I changed back to my Martin and sang *Wandering Traveler*, the song I wrote about walking into the Roadhouse for the first time.

When I finished, I turned to change guitars again to my electric Gibson. Ed stepped into the spotlight with me and shouted, "Miss Cecily Buchanan!" into the microphone. The audience was clapping, cheering, and stomping their feet.

I turned to the band, and launched into the opening rift of *Dance All Night*. After the second rift, they came in on time, and I turned to the mic to sing.

It's been a lousy day
Come home to get away
Boss was a jerk, always down
on me
Need to kick loose and move
to feel free

Going to go out and
Dance all night
The music makes things right
Shake my ass and forget
Ain't heard last call yet
Dance all night

Boyfriend called and moaned
Says he has to work 'til dawn
Thinks I'm too dumb to catch
on
He's gettin' some on the side
I ain't staying home while he
rides
Don't want to sit around
bored

*Short dress and fuck-me
shoes, hit the door*

*Going to go out and
Dance all night
The music makes things right
Shake my ass and forget
Ain't heard last call yet
Dance all night*

<guitar solo>

*Don't want to sit around
bored
Short dress and fuck-me
shoes, hit the door
Flirt with all the good lookin
guys
Gonna find one to make me
fly*

*Going to go out and
Dance all night
The music makes things right
Shake my ass and forget
Ain't heard last call yet
Dance all night*

When I finished, I did think the roof would come off. It was a new song, one I started thinking about in New York and finished in London. It had a dance beat, and the lyrics were inspired by all the women I saw alone in the clubs. I had practiced it with the band, but no one else had heard it. Neither Darlene nor Terrie had great singing voices, but when we practiced it we decided they should come in on the chorus.

When we finished our set, we came off the stage and the headliners, two women about twenty years older than I was, intercepted me.

"Go back out there," the taller one said. "Do an encore."

"I'm not supposed to," I told her. "The contract specifically says not to." There were reasons for that. Promoters don't want introductory acts usurping the main show, and often the big stars are such divas that they would blow a gasket if they felt they were getting upstaged.

"Screw the contract," she said. "Go do something. They're going nuts out there, and you deserve it." She turned me around and gave me a shove. So I sang one more song, a quiet one, and then left the stage.

Chapter 23
Jake

Myra and I watched Cecily's performance from backstage. I could tell she was nervous, but when she walked out there and the spotlights hit her, she played with all of the confidence I was used to seeing. Compared to the elegant gowns she wore for her classical tour, she dressed for this performance in a sleeveless red wrap blouse, blue jeans and cowboy boots.

Myra was nervous, too, and clung to my arm through the first few songs. When it became evident that the audience loved Cecily, Myra relaxed and let me go, moving a few steps away with a flush on her face. During the week that she stayed with us in Greeley, I caught her watching me on several occasions, and took pains not to get too close to her when we were alone.

Cecily and the band sang a song I hadn't heard before, but I instantly knew it would be a hit. By the time she hit the chorus the second time, most of the girls in the audience were trying to sing along with her.

I glanced over at Myra, and she was singing along, too. When the song finished, the arena erupted.

"Talk about a hard act to follow," a voice behind me said. I turned and saw the two women who were headlining the show.

"God, did you ever hear a voice like that?" the other woman said.

I stayed with Cecily that night in Denver, and she was so excited that I thought she would never wind down. I don't think I could have kept up with her when I was nineteen, let alone at my advanced age of thirty.

"God, Jake," she said, cuddling up against me after we made love for the third time. "I wish you could come with me. You have no idea how much I miss you when we're not together."

"If you're like this after every performance, I'm not sure my heart is strong enough," I teased.

She giggled and put her hand between my legs. "I think your heart is just fine. It seems to be able to pump enough blood to keep this hard." I groaned as she started doing something to try and make it hard again.

She and the band took off for Santa Fe the next morning, and I went home to Greeley.

~~~

CHAPTER 24
Cecily

Maybe it was because Jake was so much closer than when I was in Europe, but I missed him a lot more on that tour. We Skyped every night, but sleeping alone in a strange hotel room afterward was incredibly lonely.

The tour was turning into a major success, and *Dance All Night* passed the two hundred thousand download mark by the time we reached Washington, D.C. Tim was already talking about recording a second album and setting up a tour for the following year.

Unfortunately, as we reached the large cities on the east coast, the paparazzi and the tabloids descended on us. One morning I was treated to a story calling *Dance All Night* an autobiographical song. They dredged up all the garbage they printed when I was in Europe with Jake. The story went on to speculate that the reason I had "called off her engagement with Jake McGarrity" was due to his cheating on me.

To say that I was angry would be putting it mildly. I could handle them intimating I was a slut, but to say anything about Jake's character was going too far. I talked to a lawyer, and he said that because of the way they couched their language, reporting "rumors" and not directly saying any of it was true, there was little I could do about it. There wasn't any way I could prove that they made up the rumors so that they could report them.

We bypassed Baltimore on purpose. Kerrigan, Jake and I felt that was an unnecessary risk. Four FBI agents were now under indictment, and the federal task force was playing havoc with the drug business there. But I did perform in Washington, and then in Philadelphia a few days later.

I was walking down the street with Myra and Terrie near the concert hall in Philadelphia when I saw Alejandro. He was standing with a pretty blonde woman who was dressed in as little as legally possible.

"Good afternoon, Cecily," he said with a smile. "It's so nice to see you again. When I heard about your tour, I was disappointed that you weren't playing in Baltimore, but I have a lot of friends in Philadelphia, so I forgive you."

All I could do was stare at him. I felt paralyzed and my mind refused to work.

"Come now," he said, "don't you have a warm welcome for your old friend? Don't I deserve a hug and a kiss? Perhaps we could get together after your show. I have missed you. You know that, don't you?"

Myra stepped between us, blocking my view of him, and it seemed to break the paralysis. Terrie grabbed my arm and pulled me away. I stumbled, but she helped steady me, and then we were walking in a different direction. Myra was on her phone.

I heard Alejandro call in Spanish, "Don't think you can hide from me. I can find you, Cecily. I can always find you."

"Tim," Myra said, "we need security. Twenty-four-seven bodyguards on Cecily, limo transport, the whole deal. No, no, I'm not sure what's going on, but we need protection right now."

They pulled me into a crowded cafe and found a table while Myra gave Tim our location. The fog around my mind seemed to fade away, and I became aware that my friends were watching me with alarm and concern showing on their faces.

"Are you all right?" Terrie asked.

"Who was that?" Myra chimed in.

"Yeah, I'm okay," I said and started shaking uncontrollably. Myra pulled me into her arms and held me.

When the shaking subsided, I looked up into Myra's face and said, "What did Jake tell you?"

"I don't understand," she said.

"Why did you call for security so quickly?" I asked.

"You're white as a sheet," Terrie said. "I've never seen anyone look so terrified in my life."

Squeezing me a little tighter, Myra said, "I remember the discussions about the tour, and that you didn't want to play in Baltimore. At one point, Jake said that Kerrigan didn't want you anywhere near Baltimore."

I took a deep breath and pulled away from her. Looking at Terrie, and then at Myra, I said, "You can't tell anyone, ever, what I'm going to tell you. Not even Jake, or Tim, or God himself, understand? If anyone ever tries to bribe you to talk, or to sell me out, I'll double whatever offer they make."

"That sounds pretty dramatic," Terrie said, with an attempt at a grin, but I could see she was shaken.

"That guy is the number three player in the drug distribution network in the Mid-Atlantic states," I said. "He's the kingpin in Baltimore. He wants to kill me, because I know too much." I took a deep, shuddering breath. "It wouldn't be quick, though. He has a thing for me. Sexually. He's obsessed, and he tried to buy me once."

I reached out and took their hands in mine. "That's why you can't ever tell anyone. It would put you in danger. I won't even tell you his name. Just know that you need to stay away from him. If anyone in the FBI ever wants to talk to you about me, don't do it. He owns FBI agents."

"Why are you telling us this?" Myra asked.

"He saw you with me," I said. "You need to understand that if anyone tries to kidnap you, or talk you into going with them, scream your head off. Don't get in a car or go anywhere with someone you don't know. No one would ever see you again. I'm so sorry. I wish you weren't caught up in this, but there's nothing I can do about it now except warn you."

"How did you get caught up in it?" Terrie asked.

"An old boyfriend. A whole string of bad decisions. Disastrous decisions. Stupid decisions. Eddie's dead now, but his boss remembers me. He's not at this concert by accident. You heard him."

We sat there, drank tea and ate a little bit, for about two hours. Myra spoke with Tim a couple of times and I called Kerrigan. I wanted to call Jake, but I was afraid he'd drop everything and fly to Philadelphia. I couldn't endanger him. I decided that I would call him after the concert, once we headed out of town.

Tim finally showed up with several large men and introduced them as our security detail.

"Tim," I said, "send me the bill. This is outside of anything you're supposed to provide. Okay?"

"We'll talk about it later," he said.

We were hustled into a limo waiting outside, and taken to our hotel so that I could change for the show. I ate dinner in my room, and then the limo drove us to the concert hall.

I don't think I gave my best performance that night, but I don't remember it very well. The limo took us to New York immediately after the show, and Myra, Terrie and I checked into a different hotel than the one where the rest of the band and entourage were staying.

We were somewhere in New Jersey when I called Jake from the limo.

"Hi, sweetheart," I said. "Jake, I saw Eddie's boss in Philadelphia tonight. He came to the concert. He ... he threatened me. Honey, you need to be careful, okay?"

"Where are you?" he asked. "I'll be there today."

"No, Jake. I have a security team now, on duty twenty-four hours a day. We're taking precautions. I'm on my way to New York now, and I'll be fine. I just need you to be aware and take precautions, too. Okay? If anything happened to you, I'd never forgive myself. I love you, Jake. You're my world. Never forget that."

We checked into a three-bedroom suite in a business hotel in the financial district. The security team told us that we would be easier to protect if we were all in the same place. Dawn was breaking over the city by the time we settled in, and none of us was particularly sleepy. Exhausted, but not sleepy. We ordered a room service breakfast and sat back with coffee to wait.

"You know," Terrie said, "I own every album you've ever made. We're the same age, and when I was in high school, I saw you perform in San Francisco. My parents asked me what I wanted for my sixteenth birthday, and I said Cecille Buchanan tickets."

Myra seemed surprised. "You've been following her that long?"

"Oh, yes. When the concert started, this little blonde-haired girl walked out on stage, and she had the entire audience in the palm of her hand. I wanted to be you so badly. I've worked my butt off since then. You showed me that it didn't matter that I was just a girl, or that I was tiny. You've always been my hero. When I heard that someone was recruiting for violins to play with you, I flew down to LA and camped in Tim's office for days to get a chance to audition."

I didn't really know what to say. I had been successful at an early age, but it never occurred to me that someone might consider me a role model. The other girls at Peabody had always been mean and jealous.

"Cecily," Terrie said, "when you cancelled your tour three years ago, was that when you got into the drug scene?"

"Yeah," I answered. "I never did drugs very heavily, but my boyfriend was a dealer, and I got caught up in the scene."

A sudden thought struck me. Resisting Alejandro was something I'd never been able to do. I always felt like a bird facing a snake, and anything he wanted, I gave him. What if Myra and Terrie hadn't been there? A feeling of emptiness and futility swept through me, and before I understood what was happening, I started crying. They came over and sat on either side of me on the couch and both of them hugged me.

"What is it?" Terrie asked.

"I don't know what I would have done without you," I sniffled. "I might have gone with him."

Myra cocked her head and studied me. "Cecily, you were obviously terrified of him. Why would you have gone with him?"

"I always have before."

"You said he tried to buy you?" Myra said. "How could he do that?"

"Women are always for sale," I explained. "Like the girl he was with today. For the right price, you could buy her. Eddie liked the prestige of having a songbird, as everyone called me, so he always refused to sell me. But he rented me for favors or coke or traded me for other girls for a night or a weekend."

Terrie looked horrified, but Myra seemed to take it in stride. "Maybe he just didn't offer Eddie enough," she said.

"Eddie was stupid. I didn't tell him that, but twenty kilos of coke is a hell of a lot of money." At that statement, I saw shock register on Myra's face. She knew what kind of money I was talking about, enough to have kept Eddie alive.

I was beginning to feel calmer. I knew they were distracting me by getting me to talk, but that was all right. "I thought I was in love with Eddie, though, so I didn't mind if he treated me rough sometimes. I just didn't know any better. But I didn't want to be with any of the rest of them any more than I had to."

"Marcus told me about your mother," Myra said. Terrie gave her a puzzled look.

"Oh, yeah," I said. "I was definitely trained to confuse love and abuse."

That wasn't the only thing I was confused about. I looked at them. "What I don't understand is why you care. You're being incredibly supportive. More than you really have to."

I knew I'd said the wrong thing immediately. Terrie's eyes widened and her mouth fell open. I couldn't interpret the look on Myra's face.

"We're your friends," Terrie said.

"No one else ever cared about me," I said. "Except Jake. None of the other girls I've ever known wanted to be friends with me." I should have understood the warning in Myra's eyes, but I blurted it out anyway. "Is it because I'm paying you?"

I didn't see it coming. Myra jumped up from the couch and spun away from me.

"How dare you?" she said, tears in her eyes. "How fucking dare you?" She was furious, an expression with which I was all too familiar from growing up with my mother.

Terrie jumped up and stood in front of her. "Because she doesn't know any better. Don't you understand? Did you have any friends when you were modeling? Did you trust any of them?"

Whirling back to face me, Terrie said, "I know what you put up with at Peabody. I had to deal with the same kind of jealous bitches at the Conservatory. But just like Jake isn't like Eddie, Myra and I aren't like those cunts. Don't lump all women together."

"Oh, God. I'm sorry, Myra. I'm so sorry." It hit me how cruel I had been. "I didn't mean it that way. I ... I just don't know why anyone likes me. I'm such a fucking mess. I understand that I make people money, but Jake's the only person who has ever treated me nice without wanting something."

The expression on Myra's face softened. "You really don't, do you? Cecily, why do you think Jake likes you?"

For the first time, I really considered that question. I had always sort of shied away from thinking about it. "I don't know. I mean, not really. I know he likes the sex, and I make him laugh and he likes that, and he likes music. I do everything I can to try and please him."

"And why do you like him?" Myra asked, cocking her head to the side and furrowing her brow.

"Because he's kind, and he's gentle. He listens to me, and he teaches me things. He makes me laugh, and he makes me feel important. Not just because I have talent, but important just being me. He makes me feel safe. He cared for me even when he didn't know who I was. He saved my life just because I asked him to. He didn't even know me. No one ever cared about me before, only what I could do for them."

I took a deep breath. "I know that it won't last, not the way it is now. He could have a lot of women, ones who are beautiful and don't have all my problems. But I'm going to enjoy it while I have him."

Terrie shrugged. "Well, I know why you got along with that Eddie guy. You aren't very bright either. I have to hand it to you, though—you put on a pretty good front most of the time."

"Jesus," Myra breathed. She stepped forward and grabbed me by the shoulders.

"Do you really think that Jake likes you because you screw him?" Myra asked. "That's like you saying that you like him because he screws you. Are you telling me that you think Jake is a liar? Do you think that he says he loves you just to get in your pants?"

"Don't you talk about Jake like that!" I said, twisting out of her grasp. All of a sudden, I was mad as hell. "You don't know him. Jake would never do that."

The corners of her mouth crooked into a slight smile. "I don't think he would, either. I give him more credit than that. You should give yourself more credit than that. "

"Don't act stupid, Cecily," Terrie said. "It doesn't become you."

CHAPTER 25
Jake

After Cecily called me, I called her agent, Tim Cummings. I felt as though a huge hole had opened underneath me. The thought of losing Cecily made my mind go blank. I couldn't imagine a life without her.

"What the hell is going on?" I asked, trying to keep my fear and anger under control.

"I'm not sure," Tim answered. "I was hoping you could tell me. All I know is that Myra called this afternoon demanding a security team and limo for Cecily. She said some guy they ran into on the street threatened her."

"What kind of threat?" I asked. "Did you or any of your people see this guy?"

"No," he said. "By the time I got to them, none of them were talking."

"None of who?"

"Cecily, Myra and Terrie went to lunch and to do some shopping," Tim said. "They were walking to the concert hall when whatever happened, happened. They ducked into a crowded coffee shop, Myra called me, and I called a security firm I'd used before."

I could hear the frustration in his voice.

"Jake, what the hell is going on?"

I took a deep breath. "Tim, I assume you know about Cecily's hiatus from performing."

"Of course," he said. "I researched her thoroughly before I signed her. Jake, there are a lot of flakes in the music business. I've been burned before by talented people who couldn't stay sober enough to get on stage."

"Well," I said, "that break she took was because she fell in with the wrong crowd. She had a boyfriend who was into the drug scene. A dealer. She wasn't ever hooked, but definitely a bad crowd. He's dead now, but she's scared to death of his old cronies. She told me that one of them showed up yesterday."

Tim thanked me for filling him in on the reasons behind the girls' freak out, and after discussing the security arrangements he had made, promised to keep me informed. After we hung up, I called Kerrigan and we discussed the problem.

"Jake, I don't blame her for being scared," Kerrigan said. "The situation in Baltimore is pretty chaotic right now. The drug trade there has always been pretty violent, but with the crackdown that's going on, the violence has escalated. Anyone who is vaguely suspected of being an informant stands a good chance of getting shot every time they stick their head out the door. In addition, the arrests are creating power vacuums, and the various gangs are fighting for territory. The murder rate is running almost double the slaughter from a year ago."

"Maybe she should cancel the tour," I said.

"Jake, I know the firm Cummings hired. You couldn't protect her any better in Colorado. I do think that she's correct, though. I would be concerned about security once she comes home."

"I don't think someone from Baltimore is going to show up in Greeley," I said. "They'd stick out like a sore thumb. Besides, they may think they're tough, but I can take care of myself, and I can take care of Cecily."

"I'm sure your commanders said the same type of thing about a bunch of ragged jihadis in Afghanistan," Kerrigan said. "Don't make the mistake of thinking the drug pushers aren't dangerous just because they're crazy and they're not trained."

I lay awake that night thinking about what Kerrigan said. The following day, I swung by the county sheriff's office on my way to work. Ted Yost had been a close friend of my father's, and I went to high school with two of his sons. The older one joined the Marines and hadn't come back from Iraq. Ted and I had a chat, and he promised to alert his men. Any big-city-looking Latinos in rented cars would get extra scrutiny from his deputies.

Then I called Dave Thomas and asked him to meet Cecily in Boston and take over directing her security.

Chapter 26
Cecily

There weren't any more incidents as we moved from New York to Boston, to Chicago and then out to the West Coast. When I was a child star, I always had security when I performed, so it wasn't difficult for me to adjust to my new restrictions.

Myra chafed at having a bodyguard follow her around when she went out in the evenings. After Chicago, she stopped hitting the clubs unless Terrie and I went with her. Since I wasn't looking for hookups, the security team didn't bother me, but I think the situation put a damper on Myra's enjoyment.

It did get better after Dave showed up. At first I was irked that Jake sent Dave without consulting me, but once I settled down, I was glad he did it. With Dave organizing things, the security personnel seemed to fade into the background instead of being at my elbow every time I turned around.

By the time we hit Los Angeles, I was tired. I just wanted the tour to be over so I could go home and be with Jake. It helped that he flew in the afternoon after we did.

Other than my time in the recording studio earlier that year, I hadn't been in Los Angeles since I was twelve years old. Jake laughed when I told him that.

"We might have been here at the same time," he said.

"I'm glad we didn't meet then," I answered. "I had enough problems dragging you into my bed without memories of me as a little girl."

I wanted to go to Disneyland, but everyone talked me out of it. Terrie looked up the attendance figures online. The day before, the population of Disneyland was almost as large as the whole city of Greeley.

"Do you really want to go there and stand in line all day?" she asked.

We did go to the Getty Museum, and out to Catalina Island. And I went shopping with Myra and Terrie on Rodeo Drive. Jake didn't go on that trip with us.

The Hollywood Bowl is a natural amphitheater, though greatly enhanced with an acoustic shell around the stage and a world-class sound system. Tim planned to record the whole show and try to sell it to public television. It was definitely the largest venue I had ever played, with a seating capacity of almost eighteen thousand, and the show sold out.

We started with the twelve songs off my current album, then launched into *Dance All Night* and the songs we planned to record for the next album. After two months playing together, the band was tight, and the huge audience fed us so much energy. We were excited and gave a solid performance that had the place rocking. At the end, we were still riding such an adrenaline high that we did five encores.

We flew back to Colorado the following day. It was two months before the country tour with Jared's band, and I told Myra that I didn't want any interviews, appearances, or anything else. I just wanted to go back to playing at the Roadhouse and sleeping with Jake every night.

That night, after a long shower together, we fell into bed and just held each other. I thought about the time I spent on the road and then coming back to the hominess of being in Greeley. I suddenly realized that the storybook dream I had been living for the past year was my reality. I couldn't have been happier.

~~~

CHAPTER 27
Jake

While Cecily was on tour, I kept her up to date on the progress of the recording studio. I couldn't claim much in the way of credit. Jared had never used his degree, but having a structural engineer oversee the construction was a blessing. Since the engineer was also a musician who planned to use the studio, I didn't worry about whether things were done correctly.

The last of the equipment and electronics were installed the week before Cecily's final performance in Hollywood. The morning after we arrived home, Jared and I took her out to inspect the studio. The look of delighted wonder that filled her face when Jared turned on the lights caused both of us to smile like a couple of fools. She and Jared spent that entire day recording songs and playing with the equipment.

Myra rented an apartment in Denver, but came up to Greeley a couple of days a week to work with Cecily. Terrie had gone back to San Francisco, but was making plans to move to Colorado. Marcus set up an audition for her with the Colorado Symphony in Denver, and she won a position as third-chair violinist. The rest of the band scattered, but all of them signed up to play on Cecily's next album.

My father had expanded the old ranch house built by my grandfather. The upstairs had six bedrooms and four baths, so we had plenty of room for Myra and Terrie when they came to visit. Cecily told me that she'd never had girlfriends before, and she still wasn't sure how to act with them. I thought it was rather odd that she kept asking me for advice. I knew as much as most men do about women and relationships between women. Practically nothing.

It was so good to have her home. I wanted to touch her all the time. The house came alive when she was in it. I felt like one of the dogs. They followed her everywhere, and so did I.

One Saturday morning, Cecily woke me up wanting to make love and was rather insistent about it. Of course, I did my best not to disappoint her.

"Jake," she said afterward, "I was talking to Jeri at the bar last night, and she offered to take Myra and Terrie and me for a drive up to Granby tomorrow. Sort of a girls' day out. Would you mind? It would give you a quiet day instead of having a houseful of gossipy women."

"No, I don't mind," I said, smiling and hugging her close. "It should be a beautiful drive. I'm glad you're making friends now," I said. "I know Greeley isn't very exciting, and I work all the time."

"I like Greeley," Cecily said. "I missed you when I was on tour, but I missed Barney and Mari and Maggie, too. I love this house, and I like the people at the bar. I wish my mother were more like Kathy. And this winter, when I get through with the tour, I'd like to spend a bit more time in Denver. We can go to the symphony, see some operas and ballets. Maybe go out to dinner and go dancing. Wouldn't you like that?"

"Yes, I would like that." I kissed her, and then she took me in her hand, then her mouth, and escalated things. We didn't do much talking after that until we got up to shower and go meet Myra and Terrie for lunch.

After lunch, Cecily announced that she was taking her friends shopping.

"If you're going to hang out in Greeley, you need to dress properly," she said with a mischievous twinkle in her eye. "There will be some hot cowboys here tonight, and you want to dress to impress, right?"

When they came back around five o'clock, Myra and Terrie wore tight, form-fitting western shirts, boot-cut jeans and cowboy boots. And hats. Their jeans looked as though they were painted on. I had to admit they looked really good.

Cecily played through the dinner hours, and we waited for her before ordering our own dinner. After she finished her last set, she thanked the audience, as she usually did, then made an announcement.

"A couple of my closest friends are here tonight. Now, I know some of you boys know how to dance without murdering a girl's feet. They're both single, so don't be shy about showing them a good time. I've told them that Colorado cowboys are the friendliest men in the world, so don't make a liar out of me. Terrie, Myra, stand up so that they know who you are."

The girls looked both pleased and distinctly embarrassed.

"Come on, stand up. Let everyone see your pretty faces," Cecily insisted.

Her friends stood and waved at everyone.

"There ya go," Cecily crowed. "Treat them as though you remember the manners your mamas tried to teach you, okay? They both have big mean brothers."

The crowd laughed.

She walked over to the bar as Jared and the band took the stage.

"You can be so shy and demure sometimes," I said, shaking my head as I handed her a glass of wine.

"I am," she said, "except when I get on stage. You want everyone to have a good time, don't you?"

I laughed. "You just embarrassed the hell out of your friends."

"Only a little bit. They'd be a lot more embarrassed if they sat there all night and no one asked them to dance. I'm starving. Are we going to have dinner now?"

~~~

CHAPTER 28
Cecily

The week before Labor Day, Jake was in town running around trying to get everything ready for the big bash we were throwing at the bar. Jared and I were leaving for our country tour of the South the following week, and we talked Jake into throwing a party.

Besides me and Prairie Lightning, Jared's band, we had three more fairly big name acts coming in. The alfalfa field beyond the parking lot had been mowed, and we set up a large bandstand in the field. Jared and the band dug a pit large enough to roast a whole cow on a spit. We had a semi-truck full of kegs of beer parked behind the bar. Dave Thomas promoted it all over Northeastern Colorado, and sold five thousand tickets. We had no idea what the walk-up traffic would be the day of the event.

I stayed home to clean house. Terrie and Myra were driving up from Denver, and Jake's Aunt Tilly was coming in with her family from out around Fort Morgan. I hadn't met any of Jake and Jared's relatives, so I was a bit nervous. We would have a full house, and the plan was to put the kids, Tilly's four grandchildren, out in the barn. I found myself wondering what the place would be like when Jake and I had kids. Knowing Jake and Jared, I could imagine that the ranch was a great place to grow up.

I heard Barney start to bark. Not his bark when Jake or Jared came home, but the way his bark sounded when strangers came to the house. I wandered over to the dining room window and peeped out. A large shiny new blue car came down the drive. It slowed, then crawled into the yard between the buildings. I didn't recognize it. Most of the people we knew drove pickups.

I went back into the kitchen and grabbed a towel, drying my hands as I walked back into the dining room.

The car came to a stop, and I tried to see through the windshield who might be coming to visit.

It was Alejandro.

I stood frozen for a moment, then ducked into the living room. I locked the front door and threw the deadbolt.

Oh, my dear God. What was I going to do? I felt a bit lightheaded and forced myself to take a deep breath. Jake had guns in the house, but they were all locked up, and I wouldn't know what to do with a gun even if I had one. I felt for my knife, even though I knew it was hanging around my neck. Taking stock of what I had, I checked my phone in the pocket of the shift I was wearing. Other than the shift, the only clothes I had on were my panties. I was barefoot.

Barney was still barking. I snuck a peek out the window, and saw that Alejandro and the others in the car just sat there.

Grabbing my sneakers and socks from the foyer, I pulled them on as quickly as I could. I knew I wouldn't be able to run in cowboy boots. Peeking out the window again, I saw someone stick their hand out of one of the car windows. The sound of the gunshot made me jump, and I felt as though my heart stopped for a moment.

Barney let out a scream and twisted in a strange way. The gun fired two more times, and Barney lay in the dirt with a pool of blood around him. Mari took off running for the stable.

My heart hammered in my chest. Rushing to the back door, I set the locks, including the one on the dog door, and slipped out. I tried to pull the door closed as quietly as I could. Crouching, I snuck toward the corner of the house. I was blocked from Alejandro's view, but there would be a brief time that I was exposed between the house and the stable. If I was lucky, I could do it without anyone seeing me.

I wasn't sure how many of them were there. Alejandro for sure, and the driver. I thought the gun had been extended from the back seat, but with the angle I had, I couldn't be sure. I decided I should assume there were four of them. Any more, and they would have brought another car.

A part of me was planning, and another part was panicked so bad that I could barely breathe. I couldn't see them, and they couldn't see me. They might think no one was home. There weren't any cars in front of the house. I didn't know if they would send someone around to the back door, but I didn't think I could stay where I was and take the chance.

The shift I wore was an old one of Mary's. Once it had been bright yellow, but was now faded with age. It probably hit her above the knee, but on me it hung to mid-calf. I worried that it might tangle around my legs when I ran so I pulled it up above my knees and tied a knot in it. Then I pulled my knife out and held it in my hand.

I heard car doors slam. Lying down, I edged my eye around the corner of the building, trying to expose as little of myself as possible. I didn't see anyone.

Through the open window above me, I heard someone pounding on the front door. Jumping up, I sprinted toward the far end of the stable. As I passed through the open space where someone near the car might be able to see me, I chanced a look toward the car and saw a man's back. My breathing and the blood pounding in my ears sounded as loud as a freight train, and I was sure Alejandro and his goons could hear it, even though they were a couple of hundred feet away from me.

I peered around the corner of the building and didn't see anyone coming toward me. I did hear them hammering on the front door of the house, and then a crash, and then silence.

The copse of trees around the stream and the swimming hole where Jake and I picnicked was visible in the distance. Jake said it was two miles from the house. On horseback, it took us about half an hour to reach it, but we rode slowly. I had walked it a few times, and it took me about the same amount of time. If I ran straight toward it, no one would be able to see me from the house unless they were in Jared's or Mary's rooms on the second floor. The stable blocked the view from ground level.

I took out my phone and found Jake's number, then started jogging toward the trees. When I was far enough away that I was sure no one could hear me, I punched the call icon.

"Hi, sweetheart," Jake said. "What's up?"

"Jake, there are men from Baltimore at the house. They have guns. Call the police." My speech probably sounded a bit strange. I was panting and the pounding of my feet on the ground gave what I was saying a sort of cadence.

"Where are you?" All the playfulness was gone from his voice.

"I'm running toward the swimming hole," I told him. "I think I got away without being seen."

"Yes, that's a good idea," he said. "When you get there, go west. The banks of the creek deepen and start to wind in that direction. It will be harder to see you. I'm about ten miles from home, hang on and I'll be there as soon as I can."

"Jake, no. Call the cops. Jake, they … they shot Barney." My voice hitched a little bit when I said that. He was such a sweet dog. I wanted to cry, but focused. "Jake, they didn't see me. They can't know for sure that I'm here. Be careful. Wait for the cops. If anything happened to you, I'd die. Please, oh please don't do anything stupid."

"Okay," he said, "I'll call the police, then I'll call you back. How many of them are there?"

"Jake, no. I'll leave my phone on and lock it. That way you can hear me. Call the police on your other line. I can't talk and run at the same time, but you'll be able to hear me. I'll tell you what's happening. Okay?"

"Yes," he said. "Hide, Cecily. Hide and I'll come for you. How many men are there?"

"I saw three, but I think there are four. I love you, Jake," I said. Muting the speaker but leaving the call open, I locked my phone and slipped it back in the pocket of my shift.

Looking behind me, I didn't see anything. I slowed to a walk while talking to Jake, but now I started jogging again. It didn't seem as though the trees were getting any closer. How far away did I need to be from the house before I was out of range? I had read somewhere that a person never heard the gunshot that killed them. Bullets travel faster than the speed of sound. I wondered if I would know if I was killed, or if it would be like turning off a light switch.

~~~

CHAPTER 29
Jake

Cecily's call put me into a panic. I was driving toward the house already, and I pushed the gas pedal to the floor. I called 911, but I had no plans to wait for the sheriff's department to catch up to me. There might not be a deputy within twenty miles. Weld County is huge, almost four thousand square miles, and Ted Yost's force wasn't large enough to cover it all.

The 911 dispatcher took the information I gave her, but then Ted came on the line before I could hang up.

"Jake, don't do anything stupid," he said.

"Ted, I'm not going to rush in there, but I'm not waiting for your deputies before I scope things out. That's my girl, and if there's a way to get her out of there, I'm going to take it."

"Dammit, Jake. This isn't Iraq. Wait for backup."

"Ted, thanks for admitting I have a right to be there," I said and hung up.

I switched back to the other line, the one Cecily said she would leave open. All I heard was static and swishing noises. I listened for a while, and finally heard what sounded like a soft curse. It was Cecily's voice. Then more swishy noises.

From what she told me, all of the thugs were at the ranch house. I should be able to drive most of the way to the house without being seen. Most of the area was flat, but the area to the north of the house had a couple of low hills. Not really even hills. They were so low even my grandmother could climb them when she was eighty. But Granddad built the house where he did to take advantage of those pimples on the plain to block the north wind.

I pulled the truck off the road at a windmill about three hundred yards from the house. Reaching in the glove box, I pulled out my Glock, checked it, and jacked a shell into the chamber. There were three long guns locked into the rack behind my head. A shotgun and two rifles. I used the .308 to hunt deer and elk, and the .244 for coyotes and antelope. The advantage of the lighter rifle was that it was very flat shooting, good for long distances. I took it and the shotgun and relocked the .308 in the rack.

Circling around the hills, I came on the ranch from the north. It seemed as though the hike took me forever, but when I checked my watch, it had only been five minutes since I left the truck.

Carefully peering over the top of the rise, I looked down on the house and outbuildings. I was about a hundred yards away, and I could see the car Cecily described. The front door of the house stood open, and Barney lay in the driveway. Bright red blood covered his side, and a dark spot surrounded him.

Three men wandered around, one on the front porch, another near the car, and the third stood next to the open stable. I pulled the rifle to me, cautiously putting it to my shoulder, and looking through the telescopic sight. Everything I had seen before leaped closer, but I didn't see anything new or different. As much as I itched to do something quickly, I took a full minute to listen. Nothing. I wasn't sure if I was too far away, or there wasn't anything to hear.

I used the scope to look beyond the ranch buildings in the direction of the creek. The first thing I saw was a man dressed in dark clothing walking in that direction. He had covered about half the distance. Farther on, I saw something yellow moving away from me. Cecily had a good lead on him, but obviously he had spotted her and was following.

At that distance—over a mile—I had absolutely no shot. I would need to take care of the men at the house before I could pursue Cecily and the man hunting her.

It had been three years since I last lined up a man in the crosshairs, but six years as a sniper in Iraq and Afghanistan isn't something you quickly forget. No matter how much you might want to. I calmed myself, trying to push the fear and rage aside. I wouldn't do Cecily any good if I couldn't control myself enough to function.

Briefly, I considered the issue of shooting a man who wasn't directly threatening me. I might put Ted Yost and the district attorney in a tough spot. But Barney's body was enough to show the thugs' intent, and protecting a man's property and his woman would be enough that no jury in this county would convict me.

I set the crosshairs on the chest of the man next to the car. Taking a deep breath, I let half of it out and then held my breath. No matter how much urgency I felt, I squeezed the trigger slowly.

He spun away from me to his left and fell face down next to Barney. That motion told me that either I jerked a little when I fired, or that the slight breeze had affected the bullet.

Jacking another cartridge into the chamber, I sighted on the man next to the stable. Both of the remaining men were looking around, trying to figure out where the shot came from. I was far enough away that they couldn't really tell the direction of the sound of the gun. I placed the crosshairs on the middle of his chest and squeezed off another round.

He flew backward into the stable. Looking at his body through the scope, I could see a small splash of red in the middle of his chest.

I scanned for the third man, but he had disappeared. It took all of my will power to sit where I was. My instinct was to rush down there, hunt him out, and then go looking for Cecily. But my training told me to sit tight and wait him out. The chances were that he would crack before too much longer. He didn't know where I was, and the pistol he had wasn't made for long distances.

The time stretched, and I could still hear the swishing sounds coming from my phone. A glance at my watch told me that it had been almost thirty minutes since Cecily called me. If she was all right, she should be getting near the creek. The rifle's scope was useless at that distance, so I couldn't see her any more.

Eventually, the waiting got to be too much for my target. He poked his head out of the house, cautiously looking around. I took my time, and then took my shot. I thought of how upset Cecily would be at the mess in the foyer. I wondered if I could clean it up before she saw it. Probably not. The cops would want to do their thing first.

Leaving the rifle, I grabbed the shotgun and took off running down the hill. Where Cecily was headed, there wouldn't be any long-distance shots. The Glock and the shotgun were better for close quarters.

I checked the men I had shot. All three were dead. A quick look about in the house showed nothing disturbed, other than the broken front door and an open, half-empty beer bottle sitting on the kitchen counter.

As I entered the stable, I heard Cecily's voice on my phone. She knew she was being followed. It took me a few minutes to saddle Lightning, but he could run a lot faster than I could. Spurring him out of the stable, I prayed I wouldn't be too late.

~~~

CHAPTER 30
Cecily

Looking back, I thought I saw someone in the distance. Because we rode the horses out to the creek so often, the trail I was following was well marked. Maybe I should have gone in a different direction, but I would have taken the chance of being seen. At least I had a good head start on my pursuer.

I wasn't sure why I only saw one man. Stopping for a moment, trying to catch my breath, I scanned the distance in all directions but didn't see anyone else. I prayed that Jake and the sheriff weren't heading into an ambush.

"Jake," I said, hoping he could hear me, "there's one man following me. That means the others are still at the ranch. Be careful, honey."

Then I took off jogging again.

I looked back as I got to the creek. The man was still following me. It was hard to tell if he was running or walking, but it didn't look as though he was any closer than before. Of course, my jogging probably wasn't any faster than Jake's walking with his long strides.

Scrambling down into the small depression to the swimming hole, I looked around and saw why Jake told me to go west. To my left, the creek meandered out into the open plains, leaving little in the way of concealment. On my right, the creek tumbled down a small hill toward me. The ground rose away from me, leading eventually to the mountains thirty miles away. I stopped for a moment to catch my breath.

"Jake, I made it to the swimming hole," I said. "I'm going to follow the stream to the west, the way you told me. As far as I can tell, there's still only one man following me. I don't know if he's getting any closer. I love you, Jake."

I started to walk around the pool and caught my knee in the shift. Looking at the short but rocky climb directly ahead of me, I realized that even with the way I tied it up, the dress would be a constant problem. I took the knife and started to cut it shorter, but nicked my leg. That wouldn't work, so I pulled it over my head and held it in front of me so I could look at it. The pockets were fairly large, and my phone bumped against my thigh as I ran.

Standing there in only my panties and shoes made me feel extremely vulnerable, and I shivered in spite of the hot day. Taking my knife, I slashed at the fabric about two inches below the pocket. Once I had a cut, ripping the thin cotton was easy. I shrugged the much shorter dress back over my head and smoothed it into place. It wouldn't encumber my legs any more.

Looking around for a place to hide the remains of the skirt, I didn't see any hiding place that wouldn't be obvious. The pool emptied via a short waterfall into the creek and continued to the east. I wadded the fabric into a ball and tossed it over the fall, watching it float away on the current.

Between novels and TV, I knew that people always walked in the water to hide their tracks when someone was following them. That was fine in theory, but even in the tail-end of summer the creek was too deep for me to walk in it. I was leaving tracks in the sand around it, and there wasn't any way to hide them. I turned and started climbing out of the depression that held the pool.

It didn't take long for me to figure out that the cottonwood and willow trees lining the banks of the stream were going to be a problem. The willows in particular were so thick in places that my only choice was to go around them. That meant either going into the water, which was knee to hip deep, or fighting my way through to the edge of the vegetation where I was visible on the flat plain.

I chose to skirt along the outside of the trees, occasionally finding trails that animals used to access the stream. Stumbling along a meandering route, I kept heading west, sometimes along the water, at other times walking along the boundary where the trees met the grassland. With no idea if I was still being followed, or how closely, any sound I heard set my heart to pounding and my panic soaring. I constantly expected to feel the club of a bullet entering my body.

I crossed the stream at a place where it was wide and shallow, and considered whether I should just find a thicket of willows and hide. But I never found a place where I felt secure enough to stop and wait. A while later, I ran into a rock bluff and had to cross back to the north side of the stream.

I was following a game trail away from the stream, having encountered a stand of willows clogging my path, when I heard a voice that froze me, sending my heart leaping into my throat.

"Cecily. How nice to see you again," Alejandro said.

I spun around and found him leaning against a cottonwood tree. He was only about ten feet away, pointing a gun at me.

"My, my," he said, a mocking grin on his face. "If I didn't know better, I would think you're avoiding me. And after I've come all this way just to see you. Is that any way to treat an old friend?"

He motioned with his other hand, crooking a finger in a 'come here' gesture. I walked toward him. As I did, I slipped the knife, hidden behind my leg in a fold of my dress, into my pocket. He moved away from the tree, and when I reached him, he grabbed me by the hair and slammed me into the trunk.

"You little bitch. Don't you know better than to run from me?" he hissed. "I should blow your fucking head off for the trouble you've caused me."

His face was only a few inches from mine. Although I was terrified, a rational sliver of my mind perked up at his threat. A wild improbable hope bloomed that perhaps there was still a chance that he wouldn't kill me.

"I was scared, Alejandro," I whispered.

"What the hell were you afraid of? That I might kill you for being a rat? You damned well better be scared."

"I'm not a rat," I said.

He slammed my head back against the tree trunk, and I saw black and then stars.

"Bullshit. I've got cops and feds all over me in Baltimore. Eddie dies and the next thing I know I have problems. Who else would cause that?"

"I don't know. It wasn't me."

"Then why did you run?"

"Because when you killed Eddie, I figured I'd be next. But I wasn't in his business. You know that. I was never in his business."

He drew back a bit. "I didn't kill Eddie," he said. "What made you think I killed Eddie?"

"Who else? He owed you money and he was playing with the feds, hoping they'd bail him out. I didn't know the guys who did it, but I figured they were yours."

"I thought you might have killed him," he said. "What do you mean 'he was playing with the feds'?"

"Driscoll," I said. "The feds caught on that Driscoll was dirty and they pressured Eddie. They busted him with ten kilos, and told him that if he played ball, they would pay you off. Otherwise, they'd let you kill him."

Driscoll was the FBI agent on Eddie's payroll. I had thought a lot about what to do and say if Alejandro ever caught up to me. I didn't know if I would ever have the chance to talk my way out, but if I did, I was going to try.

"Alejandro," I said. "If you didn't kill him, and I didn't kill him, then I don't know who did. But please, dear God, please, don't kill me. I haven't done anything," I sobbed. It didn't require any acting to show him I was terrified. The gun pressed to my chest was all too real. It was hard to breathe. I felt a dribble of pee soak my panties.

"I would be a fool to let you live, Cecily. You know too much."

"No, I don't. Oh, God, please. I don't know anything. Please. I'll do anything you want me to. I'll go with you. You always liked to fuck me. Eddie's gone. You can fuck me all the time. Please don't kill me."

"Oh, I'm going to fuck you," he said. "Whether I kill you or not, I'm going to fuck you. You're the best piece of ass I ever had."

If my phone was still working, Jake was hearing all of what Alejandro and I were saying. Part of me died thinking of that. I had lied to him, told him I would never have sex with anyone but him. A cold rage built inside me. Even if I managed to talk Alejandro out of killing me, he had destroyed what I had with Jake.

Alejandro let go of my hair and plunged his hand under my dress between my legs. Cupping my sex, he began to rub me.

"You like that, baby? Yeah, I can see you do. God, you're even wet," he said. "You always like it, don't you? I never seen a whore so hot to trot as you are. It don't matter who or where."

He put his hand inside my panties and stabbed a finger inside me. Sick pervert that I was, it felt good, even though it hurt, and I felt my juices begin to flow. It always happened. Even with that brute in West Virginia who savagely beat me and raped me, I got wet and had an orgasm. When I was gang raped at the homeless shelter in Memphis, I came so many times I lost count. I had orgasms over and over when the truck driver in Kansas tied me up and repeatedly sodomized me for three days.

"Take my cock," Alejandro said. "Take it out so I can fuck you."

Fumbling with his belt, I finally got it undone and unzipped his pants. Reaching inside, I found his hard cock. It had always seemed small, but after being with Jake, it was like a joke. I squeezed him, and stroked him, and he moaned.

His hand grabbed my panties and pulled them down even as his body pressed against me. The bark of the tree dug into my back, but that was a minor pain compared to everything else. He tried to spread my legs, but the panties around my knees prevented it. Suddenly dropping to his knees, he grabbed my panties with both hands and pulled them down to my ankles.

For the first time, the pistol wasn't pointed at me. I stared at the bare skin above his t-shirt, the soft indentation where his neck met his shoulder, outlined by his collarbone. That same soft place I had stared at as the man in Kansas City raped me in that filthy alley.

A dog barked, very close to us. Alejandro's head jerked to his left, toward the sound.

I didn't miss in Kansas City, and I didn't miss with Alejandro. Pulling the athame out of my pocket, I plunged it into that soft skin at the base of his neck, burying it to the hilt. He froze in place. For a brief instant, I had a vision of him rising from his crouch, pushing the pistol into my stomach, and pulling the trigger.

But he didn't. He leaned back a bit, then stumbled when he tried to rise, falling backward and lying on the ground, staring at me. He made a pawing motion at the knife, but his hands and arms didn't seem to work properly. His legs started to twitch, then violently kicked. A rattle of air escaped his throat, and he lay still.

The shocked expression on his face, the wide-open eyes, was the same as the rest of them. In death, they all looked the same. Eddie, the man in West Virginia, the filthy drunk in Kansas City, the truck driver in Kansas, and now Alejandro. It was jolly good fun while they tortured and raped me. None expected me to fight back.

"Jesus Christ," I heard Jake say. Turning my head to the right, I saw him standing there holding a shotgun. Mari stood by his side wagging her tail.

He rushed to Alejandro, kneeling beside him for a moment, then dropped his gun and spun toward me. I braced myself. Oh, dear God. Maybe it would have been better if I'd let Alejandro kill me. I had been lying to Jake for so long, letting him think I was a good person. Now he could see for himself what kind of monster I was.

Jake swept me into his arms, hugging me and kissing my face.

"Are you all right? Oh, God, Cecily. Are you hurt?" I could hear an echo of his voice. I realized that it was coming from his pocket. My phone was still broadcasting.

He was crying. His hands were all over me, gently checking me for wounds.

"Say something," he pleaded. "Did he hurt you?"

I took his face in my hands and kissed him. I didn't know if it was the last time I would ever get to do that, so I made it a good one. He kissed me back, and that broke me. I started shaking so hard that my legs gave way. Jake gathered me into his arms and lowered me to the ground.

"Cecily, please, love. Are you okay? Talk to me."

"I'm okay," I managed to say. "I'm so sorry. Jake, I'm sorry. I didn't mean what I told him. You have to believe me. I only told him I'd go with him so he wouldn't kill me. I'm sorry. I love you. I didn't want to fuck him." I was babbling. Babbling and sobbing and trying to kiss him all at once.

"It's okay, honey," he said. "I know you didn't mean it. You're a survivor. You did what you had to do to save your life."

I drew back and looked at his face. It was filled with worry, and with love. "You're a fool, Jake McGarrity," I said. "All I ever do is cause you problems."

He took a ragged breath. "Yeah, but I'm your fool," he said, "and you're stuck with me."

CHAPTER 31
Jake

I arrived just in time to see the man Cecily called Alejandro pull her panties down around her ankles. I was carrying the shotgun, but couldn't use it for fear of hitting her. I shifted the gun to my left hand and started to draw my Glock when she pulled that damned knife out of her pocket and struck. It was fast and clean and she didn't hesitate at all. The look on her face was one I hoped never to see again. Absolute calm combined with pure hatred.

Cecily looked more bedraggled than I had seen her since the day she first walked into my bar. Her hair was full of twigs and leaves, her legs were dirty and scratched, and her dress was little more than rags.

I tried to help her pull her panties up, but she shooed me away. Taking them off, she wadded them up and threw them into the bushes. I must have looked puzzled, because she blushed and said, "I was scared, Jake. I peed my pants. I don't want to put them back on."

I had seen combat veterans do that, so I completely understood. Hell, I almost did it a couple of times.

I boosted Cecily up onto Lightning's saddle, then mounted behind her, wrapping my arms around her and holding her close. I turned the horse and headed back toward the house.

We left the drug dealer where he died. I figured that I would let the sheriff's department clean up the trash.

We had gone about a mile when my phone rang.

"Jake McGarrity," I said when I answered.

"McGarrity. This is Deputy Tom Schafer. I'm at your place. Where are you?"

"A couple of miles away. I'll be there in half an hour," I said.

"What the hell happened here?"

"A bunch of thugs broke into my house and tried to kill my fiancée. There's another one out here by the creek. Call Don Wilson in the U.S. Attorney's office in Denver and tell him you have a bunch of Baltimore drug dealers."

"I've called the Sheriff and the ME. They're on their way," Schafer said. "Are you walking or driving?"

"Riding," I answered and hung up.

Cecily leaned back against me, one hand on the pommel of the saddle and the other over my hand wrapped around her waist.

"You found me pretty quickly," she said.

"Mari found you. I told her to 'find Cecily', and she took off running toward the creek."

When we reached the stable, I dismounted and pulled Cecily down. Mari was jumping around, trying to lick her face. She knelt down and hugged the dog, scratching her ears and telling her she was a good girl.

I took Lightning into the stable and hitched him to the post next to his stall. At the other end of the building, I could see a man in uniform, probably Schafer, standing near the body of one of the men I'd killed. Cecily started in that direction

"Cecily, no. Let's go around, sweetheart."

"Why? Do you think I'm so fragile I can't handle a dead body?" she asked, continuing on her way.

She stopped by the body and looked down at it. Then she looked up at the deputy.

"That's Ramon Torres," she said. "He's a drug dealer and enforcer from Baltimore."

Giving him a wide berth, she sidled past him out the door. I followed her.

She gave a quick glance toward the body in the yard near Barney, but didn't stop on her way toward the porch.

"Cecily, you really don't want to go in there," I called.

She ignored me, walking up on the porch and bending to look at the man lying in the doorway. He had a round hole in his forehead. The rest of his head was spread all over our foyer. I had a brief irreverent thought, wondering if insurance would replace all the coats and shoes.

"Miguel Torres, Ramon's brother," Cecily said. Then she whirled around, bouncing down the steps and coming to a halt in front of me.

Looking up at me, with a serious expression that brooked no nonsense, she asked, "What did you do in the military, Jake?"

It was the first time she ever asked me a question about my time in the service.

"I was a sniper."

Nodding, she said, "Maybe we are meant for each other."

Turning, she walked toward the third man. "Alberto Morales. The man out by the creek is Alejandro Morales. He's the leader."

Then she sat down next to Barney and pulled his head into her lap. Mari came and lay beside her, nosing at Barney's body. Tears spilled down Cecily's cheeks as she scratched Mari's ears.

"What the hell happened here, Jake?" Schafer asked.

"Cecily called me and told me that drug dealers from Baltimore were here to kill her," I said. "She ran, and one of them followed her. I took out these three, and took the horse to go look for her. The other one caught her about three miles southwest of here."

He glanced at the Semper Fi tattoo on my forearm. "And you killed him, too?"

"No, he was dead when I got there. But I would have killed him if I got to him first."

Schafer jerked, turning to look at Cecily. She looked like a little girl, sitting there in her ragged dress crying over her dog.

Ted Yost arrived shortly after we did, and the U.S. Attorney came about two hours later along with a couple of FBI agents from the Denver office. Cecily and I gave our statements, and then the FBI questioned each of us separately. I only told one lie. I said that the men I killed threatened me with their guns. No one asked me how far away I was when I shot them.

We spent the night in a motel after they finally let Cecily get some clothes from the house. At first, one of the sheriff's deputies tried to keep her from going inside, saying it was a crime scene.

With her normal contempt for stupidity, she asked him, "Do you think this outfit is attractive?" indicating her ragged, bloody dress. "I'm not very fond of it, myself. Do you need it for evidence, too? Maybe I should just take it off. There isn't anything under it. The thugs who wanted to kill me didn't give me a chance to pick out my wardrobe for the day. Just tell me what you want me to do, Deputy. I'll be a good little girl."

Ted stepped in and let her go wash and pack a bag.

~~~

CHAPTER 32
Cecily

It took a couple of days before the cops let us back in our house. When they finally did, Jake tried to leave me at the bar while he went home to clean up and meet the people who were putting in the new door. I told him that I was the reason for the mess, and I wasn't going to make him clean it up by himself.

Brave and noble words. I had seen Miguel's brains splattered all over the foyer, and it really didn't bother me that much. But I hadn't realized how much adrenaline and anger I was running on at the time. I also hadn't considered that everything would have dried in three days' time, or how bad the smell would be in the summer heat.

I really wasn't prepared for the smell. When Jake opened the door, I took one breath, then hurried over to the flowerbed and threw up. Jake was right behind me. It was sort of a bonding experience, as if we hadn't been through enough together.

He took a card out of his pocket. "Ted told me to call these people to come clean the house. I figured that I'd save the money and the insurance hassle. Maybe that was a bad idea."

"You think?" I asked. "Hell, that smell has probably permeated everything in the house."

He made the call. They had to come out from Denver, so we took the horses out for a ride. When we got back, we waited for the cleanup crew in the stable. We stayed in the hotel for three more nights, and when we came home, I had to deal with sorting out all my clothes, which had to be cleaned or laundered.

I told him no more killings in the house. I meant it as a joke, but he looked so terrible after I said it that I had to hug him and kiss him and tell him I was only teasing.

Finally, we were able to go home and resume our lives, but there was one more thing I had to do before I felt we could really go forward.

Lying in bed that night, I said, "Jake, I'm sorry I lied to you."

"About what?" he said in a lazy tone of voice.

"About killing Eddie."

He rose to a sitting position and looked down at me. "You killed him?"

"Yeah. I couldn't tell anyone, not even you. If you want to tell a really big lie, you have to make sure you never change your story. If you can convince yourself, you can convince everyone else. I probably could have passed a polygraph."

I took a deep breath. "I'm a very good liar, Jake. My mother taught me when I was very young that the easiest way to avoid punishment was to tell her what she wanted to hear. 'Yes, Mother, your new double Ds look entirely natural on your five-foot-three, one hundred and five pound frame.' 'No, Mother, your new bleach blonde hair doesn't look trashy.' 'Of course I spent the afternoon practicing, Mother. I would never dream of wasting precious time reading a comic book I stole from Tommy Martin's house.' That's why I didn't want to answer your questions. You were the first person that ever treated me with kindness, just because you thought it was the right thing to do. So I've tried my damnedest never to lie to you."

"Do you want to tell me about it?"

"Yes. I do. I want to get rid of everything that's still standing between us. And if you want me to leave in the morning, just take me to the bus station."

"You stabbed him," Jake said, and I saw his eyes shift to my knife sitting on the dresser by the door. I was surprised the sheriff's office had returned it.

"Yes, but not with that knife. I left the knife. Remember when I told you that Eddie owed some people a quarter of a million dollars?"

Jake said, "Yes."

"That was true. What I didn't tell you was that he came up with a scheme to get the money. He decided that he would move me up to New York, and then send a ransom note to my parents telling them to give him the money or he'd kill me. God, the number of holes in that plan made my head spin. Something you have to keep in mind is they don't require an IQ test to deal drugs, and Eddie wasn't that bright when he was sober."

I sat up so I could see Jake's face easier.

"Even if my parents were inclined to pay the ransom, I couldn't see them doing it without calling in the police. I received kidnapping and other threats for years. Everyone seems to think that kidnapping a child star is the road to instant riches. Then there was the problem of whether they had the money. Since they didn't have access to my trust anymore, and I wasn't performing, I wasn't sure of their financial situation. They had been living off me for years. Of course, I was never fool enough to tell Eddie about my finances, or that I had money of my own."

"What parent wouldn't try to pay to ransom their child?" Jake asked quietly.

"You met my mother. What if the child was an ungrateful, drug-addict whore?" I asked in return. "Keep in mind, if I die, my parents inherit my wealth. Or they would have then. I fixed that. I'm not saying they would have thrown me under a bus, but the ties of parent-child love were extremely strained. We had a number of shouting matches about me canceling the tour and living with Eddie."

I looked out the window, seeing the stars twinkling at me. "But what scared me the most was that Eddie really would kill me. He had been spending a lot of time with a new girl, and I wouldn't put it past him to slit my throat if my parents didn't pay. So, I tried to talk Eddie out of it. And he did something he had never done before. He hit me."

I remembered the scene so well. Eddie saying, *"I'm tired of arguing with you. We're going to do it my way. Shut up and go get me a beer."*

"Eddie, I'm telling you it won't work. We need to figure out another way."

I didn't even see the fist coming. In almost two years of abuse, of being raped and sold to other men to rape, he had never hit me. He knocked me off the bed, and I lay on the floor, confused more than hurt, trying to understand what had happened.

"Listen, bitch. You don't tell me what to do. If I say, go get me a fucking beer, you go get me a beer. Do you understand me, you fucking cunt?"

"So I went to the kitchen and got him a beer," I told Jake. "But I also brought back a chef's knife. He was lying on his back, his head propped up with a pillow against the headboard. I put the beer on the nightstand, turned, and drove the knife into him with both hands."

It entered just below his breastbone, and went all the way through to the mattress. Other than a loud gasp, he never said a thing. I left the knife where it was, wiped the handle and the beer bottle with the sheet, and went to take a shower. I discovered that even when you stab someone in the heart, there isn't much blood if you don't pull the knife out.

"All the abuse, everything he did to you, and you killed him because he hit you," Jake said.

It wasn't really a question, but I said, "Yes."

"Good for you," he said. "If every man who hit a woman got the same treatment, it wouldn't bother me at all."

I sat there waiting for something more. He reached out and cupped my face in his hand. Then he leaned forward and kissed me.

"I consider myself warned," he said. "Never hit Cecily." And then he took me in his arms and kissed me again, and again, and made love to me.

I lay in his arms later, listening to his breathing, with tears running down my face. Finally, I could allow myself to be happy.

The following day as I was getting dressed, Jake came into the bedroom and knelt in front of me. He pulled out the little box that held the diamond ring he bought when I was taken into protective custody. But when he opened his mouth, I put my hand over it. My heart was hammering as hard as it did when Alejandro stuck the gun in my chest. For an entirely different reason, of course. I was so elated that I thought I might float off the floor. But he was throwing a wrench into one of my dreams, my fondest fantasy.

"Are you going to ask me to marry you?"

He nodded.

"You really want to marry me? Do you want to have kids and all that?"

He nodded again.

My breath caught in my throat, and it took me twice to actually form the words, but I managed to keep my voice steady. "I'm not ready for that, Jake. You know I love you, but there's something I want to do first. Something I have planned, but I've been too afraid to do it. I've always been afraid that being with you is just a dream, and that I'll wake up some morning and you'll tell me to leave."

"How can you even think that?" he asked. "You know I love you. Cecily, this is real. We are real. There's never going to be anyone for me except you."

I leaned over and kissed him.

"Put the ring away, but not too far away, okay? Like I said, you've just given me the courage to do something I've wanted to do for a long time. Please let me do it?"

He stood and put the ring back in his pocket. "You know I would do anything for you. Am I going to have to wait very long?"

Pulling his head down and kissing him, I said, "No, Jake, not very long at all. Let me play my little game and then I'm yours."

We dressed and headed out with me driving. I had finally gone into town and paid for my learner's permit. It took us twice as long to get there when I drove.

That evening at the bar, I played my normal two hours. When I finished, I pulled the microphone close and said, "Jake, can you come up here, please?"

He wiped his hands and came out from behind the bar. I put out my hand and pulled him onstage. Then I knelt down in front of him and began to play.

You tell me that you love me
And you show me every day
I've never been in love before
I never knew the way
I didn't know the world could be
Such a lovely place
And I didn't know that angels had

A handsome cowboy face
I never knew that being owned
Could set you truly free
Jacob Allen McGarrity
Will you marry me?

I pulled out a small box and opened it, showing him the ring I'd commissioned from a jeweler in London. He smiled and put out his hand and I slipped the ring on his finger, then he pulled me to my feet and kissed me. The whole bar was cheering. It was exactly the way I imagined it.

###

If you enjoyed ***I'll Sing for My Dinner***, I hope you will take a few moments to leave a brief review on the site where you purchased your copy. It helps to share your experience with other readers. Potential readers depend on comments from people like you to help guide their purchasing decisions. Thank you for your time!

Author's note:
In most, if not all, states in the U.S., a 200-pound man can beat and rape a 100-pound woman and she is not allowed to defend herself using lethal force. The normal standard is: A person may use non-deadly force to prevent imminent injury; however, a person may not use deadly force unless that person is in reasonable fear of serious injury or death.

Many courts (usually male judges) have ruled that rape is not a "serious injury". She can't shoot her rapist or stab him or hit him in the head with a rock unless he is trying to kill her. And if she does kill him, she must prove her innocence and his intent.

Since most such crimes have no witnesses, such proof often is difficult. As a result, of the men Cecily killed, only Alejandro would qualify as a "justified homicide", since he had a weapon and threatened to kill her in the presence of a witness. If such laws seem insane, then public pressure should be brought to change the laws concerning violence against women.

Printed in Great Britain
by Amazon